Between

S. EVEREST

BETWEEN

By S. Everest

This book contains sensitive subjects, such as drinking, explicit sexual scenes, religious views, and graphic violence.

Other triggers are considered spoilers and will not be listed here. You can find a full list of triggers on my website: http://www.severestbooks.com/triggers

This book is meant for those ages 18+.

This book does *NOT* end in a traditional Happily Ever After.

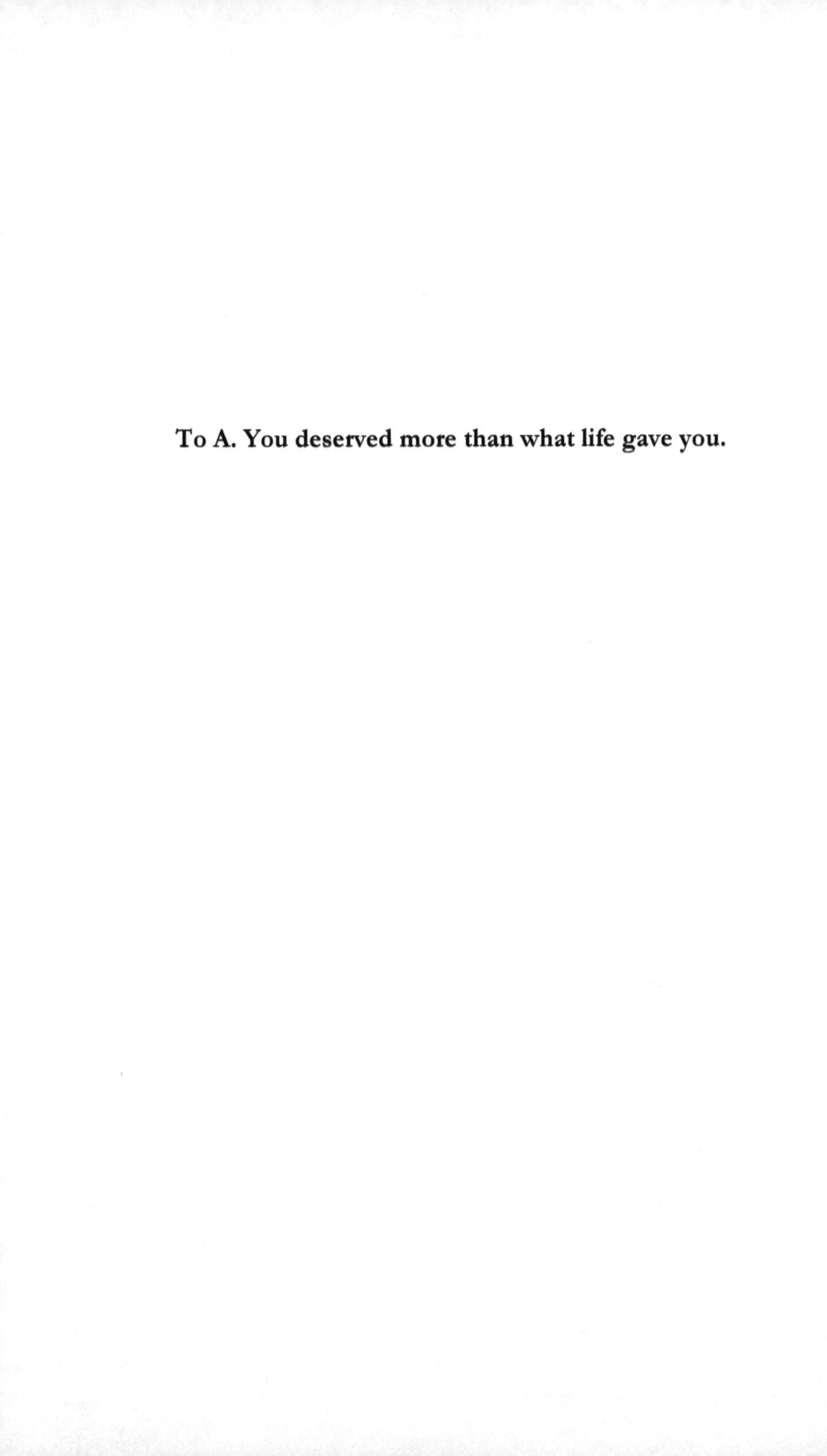

To A. You deserved more than what life gave you.

Playlist

Bleed
deadmau5

World Unknown
PhaseOne, ERRA

In The Rain
ODESZA

The Grey
Bad Omens

Tonight (demo)
Amira Elfeky

In Circles
Holding Absence

Up in Houses
Falling Up

Another You
BONNIE X CLYDE

SUPERBLOOM
Silent Planet

Ultraviolet
Spiritbox

Heavener
Invent Animate

Dead in the Water
Ellie Goulding

Hospital for Souls
Bring Me the Horizon

Glass

Burn

Red

Celeste

Rain pattered against my windshield as I pulled my car up the wet, winding road. Leaning forward, I craned my neck to get a better view of my surroundings, but the heavy fog shielded me from seeing much. With a sigh, I fell back into my seat, my hands tight on the wheel as I kept my gaze on the red taillights in front of me. I followed as they led me on a curvy path up a hill, my windshield wipers pushing heavy raindrops to the sides of my view.

The inside of the car was too quiet. I had no cell phone service, since we seemed to be in the middle of nowhere, and not even satellite radio reached this part of the planet. I pushed every button I could on my car's stereo, tried closing and restarting Spotify, and even searched around on the local radio stations, but absolutely nothing came through. So, I wallowed in silence, my black dress itching and scratching my thighs, my eyes red and burning from crying these past few days.

At least I had the steady beat of the windshield wipers to keep my sanity at bay.

With the palm of my hand, I wiped away a sudden stray tear, careful not to ruin my carefully applied makeup.

But with the single tear came an ache in my throat, one that I couldn't simply push away when I thought of the reason why I was even here.

"Celeste, baby girl! The light of my life!"

I could feel the echo of his voice in my heart, beating along with my pulse.

But that's all his words were anymore. An echo.

I knew this was going to happen. I knew I wasn't going to be able to keep it together. Thankfully, I brought along a small package of tissues that were conveniently sitting on the passenger seat. I grabbed the plastic, ripped it open, and pulled one out, dabbing the rush of tears that were coming in by the dozen, careful not to pull my makeup off with it.

The choke in my throat wasn't going away soon, and I wasn't sure how much longer we had until we got to the top. Or the end.

I can't tell because I can't see a damn thing.

The car in front of me hit the brakes, forcing me to do the same. We came to a short, rolling stop before picking up the drive again. And once we continued on, that's when the fog lifted away, and I could finally see where I was.

In front of us was a huge set of black iron gates that were propped open against tall, dark stone columns to allow all cars in. I looked up through the raindrops at the gorgeous design. There was dark green ivy twisted around the edges, snaking its way through the bars and reaching the top. The leftover fog settled at the bottom, resting on the damp road as the mysterious location granted us entry.

What kind of place is this?

An older guard stood at the open gates, a clipboard in one hand and an open umbrella in the other. He stopped the car in front of me, nodded at their words, then made his way to my car. I rolled down the window, quickly sniffled up any extra emotion, and painted a polite smile on my lips.

"Good afternoon, Miss. May I have your name?"

"Celeste Castell."

The man nodded, slowly stepping away. "Thank you."

And with that, he was gone, already making his way to the car behind me. I rolled up my window.

The short train of cars pulled in and drove higher, until we came to another older man standing on the side of the road. He lifted a hand to signal us to stop and pull over, so we did. There were two cars in front of me and only one behind me, and we all pulled off to the side and turned our engines off.

I took a deep sigh, one that expanded my chest more than what was comfortable. "Here we go," I said to no one but myself.

Reaching over to the passenger seat, I grabbed my black raincoat and put it on, pulling the hood up and tucking away my dark brown hair.

"Hey, want to go somewhere special?"

"Like where?"

"Oh, I don't know… Disney World?"

I only eyed the package of tissues for half a second before grabbing it and shoving it into my pocket.

Stepping out of my car, I was met by a tall man with golden hair holding a black umbrella that covered him from the heavy drops. He handed me an umbrella of my own, and I briefly made eye contact with him before taking it.

"Compliments of the Estates."

His rich voice was smooth on my ears as he stepped aside and made his way to the car behind me, handing the man stepping out an umbrella as well.

I opened the umbrella and raised it over my head. The rain tapped on the synthetic fabric and ran over the sides, and I was extremely thankful for the cover.

I turned and looked at the car in front of me, only to see two people standing by their doors, their umbrellas open and up, waiting for me.

My parents.

Walking up to their car, I joined them in silence. The three of us made our way over to the older man who was standing on the side of the road, waiting for us. All in all, there were only six of us gathered together, seven if you include the older man waiting for us, eight if you include the umbrella man.

Who, as I turned around to look over my shoulder, was now nowhere to be found.

So, we were back to seven.

But in my glance backward, I locked eyes with the person from the car behind me. I gave him a gentle smirk, even though I could feel my chin begin to quiver at the sight of him. *Uncle Lucas.* With soft steps and the rod of his umbrella resting on his shoulder, he approached my side, and without a word, his elbow nudged mine as a small, sympathetic grin rested on his face. I wanted to bury myself in him, right then and there, and let the fast-forming tears pour out of me.

But I collected myself and kept my composure. I can cry later.

My dad stretched across me and gave Uncle Lucas a pat on the shoulder, silently acknowledging the death of their youngest brother.

"You are all gathered here today in holy remembrance of the beloved Russell Castell," the man began, speaking over the sound of rain.

I squeezed my eyes shut at the mention of his name.

"Uncle Russ! Uncle Russ! Come play Candyland with me!"

With one hand still holding my umbrella, my other hand found its way into my pocket, my thumb gliding along the plastic tissue wrapper in an attempt to ground me.

"Will you please follow and join me at his resting place?"

The older man—who was clearly a priest based on his clothing—stepped onto a stone path, and the six of us followed. I recognized the two people in front of us; they were a husband and wife who were very close to Uncle Russ. The man was a friend since high school, and the woman was close because they were often together. I wish I could remember their names. Uncle Russ spoke nothing but good things about them, and seeing the look of sorrow on the man's face told me all I needed to know. It hurt them as much as it hurt me.

I was sandwiched between Uncle Lucas and my dad, with my mom nestled in on his other side. Her arm looped through his, her sniffles loud enough to ring through the quiet, peaceful area.

The priest led us onto a narrow walkway that had buildings on both sides. Some were small, some were massive. Some had gates, some had windows, but all had open doors. I scrunched my face at the thought. Why were they all open? Weren't the doors supposed to be closed in privacy, in respect for the deceased, in hopes they would gain peace?

As we walked, I glanced up and noticed last names on each building, and a few were so worn and faded that I had trouble reading them. Every building had greenery along the front and sides, spreading like beautiful vines in the gloomy air.

Then, the priest stopped in front of a new, large building. Tilting my head up and angling my umbrella back, my breathing stopped as I read the name above the door.

Castell.

There was no hope of keeping my tears in any longer.

An arm wrapped around my shoulders, and I leaned into it.

"It's alright, sweets," Uncle Lucas whispered to me. "It's okay."

His words were meant as a comfort, but sometimes comfort in the darkest of days only made my heart feel heavier.

"Die with the Lord in your heart, and you will gain eternal life."

The rest of the words tuned out of my head as the priest rambled on about the afterlife, soul restoration, and the comfort of Heaven above. His words fell on deaf ears as I watched him extend his arm, showcasing the gorgeous structure.

My gaze fixed on the name etched in stone as everyone else bowed their heads in prayer. Blinking lightly, another tear slipped from my eye.

"Now, Celeste, you need to go out and give 'em hell, you hear me?"

"It's only cheer practice, Uncle Russ."

"I know, but you need to show them that you're the best. Got it?"

"Got it."

My mind blocked out the prayer and the echoed textbook responses around me. I don't think I could even try to participate with the giant lump of sorrow stuck in my throat. Instead, I closed my eyes and inhaled. I needed to breathe in the wet, fresh air around me. I needed to feel the dampness on my skin. I needed to live in the life I had.

Reaching out, I opened my hand, palm up to the sky. Cold raindrops landed on my hand, filling the creases of my palm. I hoped that, wherever he was, Uncle Russ could still feel the rain.

Or, even better, he could feel the sun on his face.

On the other side of Uncle Lucas was a set of vines that scaled the side of the building. With my hand still open, I reached across him, careful not to interrupt his prayer. Taking one of the leaves in my grasp, I brushed the pads of my fingers against the smooth, flat greenery.

English ivy. A type of vine that can climb up the side of a building with no help. It lives on its own, surviving by clinging onto the nearest surface and spreading as far and wide as possible.

A brief smile appeared on my lips at the sight of nature mixed into Uncle Russ' mausoleum. It was comforting, in a way.

I dropped my hand and looked around, only to see everyone still in prayer. I briefly glanced at the other mausoleums before landing on a dark figure down the curved path. There was a man standing there, completely still, watching our burial service from afar. He was tall and broad, wearing a dark rain jacket with the hood pulled up, preventing me from seeing his face. But even though I couldn't see his face, I could feel the intensity of his stare on us. On me.

Rain dripped off the rim of his hood as he stood without any cover. I could immediately tell it wasn't the umbrella guy from earlier. Was he a guest? Was he visiting another mausoleum? Was he a friend of my uncle? His dark pants looked to be drenched as I continued to watch him, waiting to see if he wanted to come over and join the group.

But he didn't. Instead, he simply stood there as the priest rambled on, our vision caught and locked on each other, the rain running off his hood and onto his shoulders.

"Here we pray for eternal rest and mercy of the Lord."

"Amen," the group muttered, snapping me back to the service. I briefly looked to my dad and uncle, but they didn't seem to notice that I wasn't participating. And if they did notice, they didn't care.

The priest nodded and stepped to the side, allowing us privacy and access to the inside of the mausoleum. The husband and wife stepped in first, but only stayed for a short moment before exiting. They greeted us politely before heading back to their car.

My mom and dad both walked up the few stone steps and headed inside. A quick sob escaped my mom, and my heart lurched at her sadness, feeling similar emotions in myself.

But when they were inside, I looked back over to the curve in the path, only to see the mysterious man was gone.

I tilted my head curiously at the empty sight.

After a drawn-out minute, my parents came back out, and my dad made his way to me. With a quick peck on the side of my head, he whispered, "I love you so much, baby girl."

Another tear rolled down my cheek. Uncle Lucas extended his elbow to me, and I wrapped my arm around him. Dropping our umbrellas, we walked in unison up the steps and into the mausoleum.

On the inside, it was spacious. There were two stone benches, one on either side against the wall. Colorful stained-glass windows lined the opposite walls, letting in minimal light as pigmented reflections barely illuminated the concrete floor.

Beautiful stone columns rested in each corner, and a rectangular counter sat against the back wall.

And on that counter was a plain black vase.

It's hard to comprehend the fact that my uncle has been reduced to ash that can fit in a countertop container.

What once was a person who never ceased to make me laugh was now a pile of dust wrapped in ceramic.

"He loved you, Celeste. You and your sister."

My uncle's voice was soft as his words found my ears. I nodded, unable to speak.

There was never a doubt in my mind that he loved us. I know Uncle Lucas and my dad love us, too, but now it felt like there was a missing piece in our family. One that we could never fill, never get back, never let go of.

"Is she okay?"

I looked at him, momentarily confused. "Who, Serena?"

He gave a nod.

"Yeah," I took in a breath, thoughts of my sister floating through my head. She took Uncle Russ' passing just as hard as I did. "She's as okay as she can be."

"Where is she?"

"She's at home. She couldn't find a sitter."

Stillness resounded in the walls of the mausoleum as he hummed in response. We both took a moment to settle in this newfound reality, that he was gone, and that this was all we had left of him.

Unwrapping myself from Uncle Lucas' arm, I approached the granite countertop. The surface was polished and shiny, with not a single speck of dirt or dust to be seen. My finger brushed against the edge.

"This place is beautiful," I began, the catch in my voice unrelenting. "I didn't even know it existed."

Turning back to look at Uncle Lucas, I watched as he shrugged. "Most people don't."

There was a truth to his statement that I couldn't shake. We were in a hidden cemetery with no cell service and no other cars or visitors. The entrance was covered in a layer of dense fog, and I would've missed it entirely if it weren't for the other cars. Before coming here, I tried searching the place on my phone, but I didn't even know where to begin. This graveyard was covered in secrecy, and I was itching to understand why.

But my grief was heavy, heavier than my desire to figure things out.

For now.

Completely turning myself to my uncle, I eyed him. His cheeks were sunken in, the skin around his eyes was purple, and the life in his irises looked hollow.

"Are *you* okay?" I asked.

He sighed. "Oh, I will be. Don't you worry about me, okay?"

I hesitantly nodded. Both my dad and Uncle Lucas took Uncle Russ' death hard, harder than they let on. They sat together in silence in my parents' garage for three nights in a row, drinking and smoking cigars, letting only their memories do the talking. But at least they were there for each other.

And in their bond, I knew Uncle Lucas wasn't lying. I knew they both would be okay someday, even if it took longer than expected to heal.

"Ready?" he asked, looking to me.

I wasn't, but I don't think I'll ever be.

With a simple nod, I walked out with him, saying a silent goodbye to someone who shaped me into the person I am today.

And as I scooped up my umbrella, continuing my exit, I looked to my left. The man from earlier was back. His jacket was still dripping, his clothes were still wet, and his eyes were still on me.

I turned away from him and walked back to my car, even with his stare burning into my back.

Celeste

Exactly eighteen days have passed since Uncle Russ' burial, but thankfully, I remembered the way to the cemetery.

At least, I thought I did.

There was more fog on the road that seemed to appear out of nowhere, and the rain was just as heavy now as it was the last time I was here. But still, I drove up the winding road to the best of my ability, only falling off the road and driving into the dirt twice.

Upon approaching the vine-covered gates, I stopped my car in front as the fog slowly dissipated.

The gates were shut.

With my eyebrows slanted down and my eyes squinted, I sat in my car, confused.

It was daylight. It was a Tuesday.

Did I miss something? Were they closed? Was there another memorial service going on?

There was no one around to even ask. There was nothing to look up on the internet to check.

I couldn't even *connect* to the internet right now.

After quickly pulling my hood up over my head, I opened my car door, stepped one foot out, and glanced around. There didn't seem to be anyone on the grounds. No private burials. No services. No one.

"Hello?" I lifted my voice louder than usual while tucking my dark brown braid into my hood.

Rain tapped against my jacket and dripped onto my jeans as I waited for a response.

"Hello?" I tried again, and finally heard a sign of life off to the side. Behind one of the stone pillars connected to the gate, the click of a door echoed through the air. A man stumbled out wearing a rain jacket and a broad smile. He was older and smaller but seemed chipper.

"Can I help you, miss?"

It was the man from the last time I was here, the one with the clipboard that took my name.

"Hi," I began, still standing slightly out of my car. "I was hoping to bring some flowers to my uncle."

The man stared at me, his smile unwavering.

There was a brief silence passed between us before I continued, my voice carrying over the rain. "Today is his birthday."

There was a sound of another car rolling up the hill, and within seconds, it was breaking through the leftover fog from the drive. The older man instantly walked over to his booth, reached in, and pressed a button. The gates opened, and the silver car drove through without stopping. I couldn't see who was driving through the heavy stream of rain, but whoever it was seemed to be known, or even belong here.

The older man came back to me and nodded, resuming our conversation as if we weren't interrupted. His smile faded. "I'm so sorry, miss, but unfortunately, we cannot let anyone in without an appointment."

"What?" The word rang out with more disbelief than I intended. "An appointment?"

"Yes," he replied, suddenly looking uncomfortable. "This is private property. Visits are by appointment only."

Rain continued to fall around us as I stood there, shocked by the new information. This was a cemetery that was closed to the public? How was I supposed to make an appointment when I didn't even know the name of the place or how to find it online? And who just drove in *without* an appointment?

Just as I was about to accept my fate and get back in my car, a voice stopped me.

"Let her in."

Both the man and I looked to the direction of the voice, which came from one of the stone pillars. There was a large black intercom speaker attached to the side.

The older man shuffled his way to the speaker, pressed a button, and responded. "She doesn't have an appointment, Sir."

"Let her in," the voice replied, this time more forcefully, sending a chill through my body.

The older man surrendered. "Yes, Sir." He turned to me, the bright smile pasted back on his face, and motioned to the gate. "Very well. You may enter."

He made his way back into his booth, and after a second, the gates opened. A piece of me was briefly hesitant, but I pushed the feeling away as quickly as it appeared. All I wanted to do was go to my uncle's mausoleum, give him his flowers, wish him a happy birthday, then go. I didn't need to wander the grounds or stick my nose where it didn't belong. I just wanted to visit my uncle.

I slowly eased my car past the wrought iron gates and pulled off the side of the road. Judging by the large, dark cloud above, the rain didn't seem to be letting up anytime soon. Turning around, I reached into the backseat to grab the umbrella that... wasn't there.

I must've left it at home. *Shit.*

Whatever. I tucked the loose strands of hair into my hood, made sure my jacket was zipped, grabbed the small bouquet of flowers from my passenger seat, and stepped out of my car.

And now that I was looking at this cemetery with eyes that weren't blurred with tears, I could see how incredibly beautiful it was.

Along with the dreary sky, every building and stone statue was a shade of grey. Grey mausoleums, grey stone walkways, and grey cement benches along the path. But in between each shade of grey, there was heavy greenery. Ivy twisted between each resting place, between every crack in the path, and along the legs of the benches. Moss covered the sides of some mausoleums, large trees shaded the trails, and shrubs and bushes were scattered throughout, all adding life in color.

And suddenly, a part of me wondered where I wanted to be when I died. Could I rest in a place like this? Could I have peace in an area so rich in life, so lush and vibrant in its green color?

Rows upon rows of carefully sculpted mausoleums lined the paths, looking like a small village of houses. There were potted plants at each one, and statues and columns between buildings. My walk took me past a large sculpture of a crying angel, with his wings spread wide and his head buried in his arms. The carved stone had to be at least twenty, maybe even thirty feet tall, hovering over the entire grounds and all the mausoleums surrounding it. I paused, my eyes glued to the image, my heart reaching for the angel. I knew that feeling. The feeling of loss, the life that has been changed, the soul that felt cracked and broken.

"An angel of grief," a dark voice spoke out to me, causing me to jump, and I turned to it. I knew that voice. It was the voice from the speaker box at the gated entrance.

Not only did I recognize the voice, but I recognized *him* as well. It was the man from the burial service, the one who watched from afar. My eyes scanned him; his pants were wet once again from the rain, his black jacket was dripping, and his hood covered his shadowed face. His hands were shoved in his pockets as he took one step toward me.

"What?" I managed to squeak out, caught off guard by his sudden appearance.

He looked up and motioned to the statue before me, and my eyes caught a glimpse of his dark profile. "It's an angel of grief."

There were no words for me to say, so he continued.

"Angels are said to have little to no emotion, but they can feel intensity. This angel," he said, lifting a hand to the statue, "can't feel sorrow, but he can experience loss. And that's the closest thing to emotion that can shatter a soul."

I took his words and rolled them around in my mind. "But if they can't feel emotion, can they have a soul?" I asked, surprising myself and feeding into the conversation, unsure as to why.

"Depends. What's a soul?" he inquired curiously.

Turning my face back to the statue, I inhaled, taking a moment to think. "An identifiable living presence."

A slight smirk lifted through the shadows that cradled his face, lighting an unknown spark in me. "That's vague," he paused, "and incredibly inaccurate."

"I'm sorry?" I cinched my eyebrows and turned to face him completely. My hand reached up to my hood to make sure it stayed over my head, keeping my face and hair dry.

His hueless eyes looked down at my flowers before coming back up to my face. "Carnations. Easily identifiable and once living."

His shoulders leaned into my direction.

"Soulless."

I looked down to the flowers in my hands, unable to find any words to respond with. The petals were an off-white color with dark red along the edges, and the stems were a dull green. They were gathered neatly in a black bow, which was beginning to soak from the rain.

I've loved carnations ever since I was a little girl. My mom would plant them next to the steps on our front porch, where I could see them every day as I would come and go. They reminded me of home, of family, and of life.

"Try again," he requested, snapping me back to the conversation. "What's a soul?"

Looking up from my flowers, I stared at him deeply as I struggled to find the answer I wanted. My eyes connected with his, my vision fighting to see the color of his irises.

"A soul is…" my words tapered off as my stance on the matter faltered. "…a connection?"

He raised his eyebrows at my answer. "A connection to what?"

I bit my bottom lip, drawing it in between my teeth. "To the world. To each other."

His head tilted at my response, and he took one step closer, erasing any gentleness from his expression. "So, then you believe your soul will always be tied to this world, or someone on it?" He took another step, and suddenly my lungs stopped working. "Do you believe that you will always need to depend on something to live? To thrive? To feel?"

At this point, he was standing right in front of me, with the rain still rolling and beading off our jackets. I looked up at him as he looked down at me.

"What's your soul feeling right now? At this very second?"

Swallowing down my emotions, I pulled out the most generic answer I could think of. "Grief. It's why I'm here."

He gave a single nod, and it was a slow movement that implied he didn't fully believe me.

After a brief pause, he protested. *"Your uncle* is the reason why you're here. Your grief is simply an emotional reaction to the loss. Your emotions didn't force you into the car and drive you here."

My lips gently parted at his claim. He was calling me out, insinuating I was lying, even if his words were subtle.

"Now, give me your real answer."

My eyes searched his with a desperation I couldn't shake. There was a forcefulness to his demand, a light growl in his words. He could see right through me, and we both knew it.

But I wasn't going to let my guard down because I didn't even *know* him.

"That *is* my real answer."

And with that, he bowed his head and took a step back. There was no rebuttal, there was no challenge. He simply took my answer as what it was.

But I knew that he still didn't believe me.

"How did you know he was my uncle?" I asked, my words hushed under the steady patter of raindrops.

With both hands back in his pockets, he rocked back on his heels. "Celeste Castell. Daughter of Victor and Meredith, sister of Serena, and niece of Lucas and Russell Castell."

"How did you—"

"Russell Castell. Died twenty-two days ago from pancreatic cancer, laid to rest here eighteen days ago."

My thoughts, my emotions, and my words were all stuck in the bottom of my throat, and he took that as a sign to continue.

"I knew you would be back, and I knew it would be today."

"How did you know?"

"Because today's his birthday."

"I… How…" My words fumbled out of me with no chance of any structure. I couldn't manage to form a cohesive thought, so I deflected. "Do you memorize all the dead people's birthdays?"

A smooth, dark chuckle escaped him as he shook his head. "No."

"Then why him?" I asked, then immediately shook my head. "No, *no*. I have a better question. Why do I need an appointment to come here? Isn't that against common cemetery rules? Isn't anyone allowed to come here at any time to pay respects to their loved ones? I mean, *someone* drove in here before me without needing one."

He raised a dark eyebrow at my questions. "This isn't a cemetery, Celeste."

"What? What do you mean? And how do you know me?" I asked. I could feel the heat rushing to my face as my voice grew louder and my tone filled with accusations I couldn't articulate.

"This is not public grounds. This is private property. The deceased who rest here have chosen to do so."

"Including my uncle?"

"Including your uncle."

"Why on Earth would he want to be here? If this isn't a cemetery, then what makes this place so special?"

The rain continued to fall between us as our eyes remained fixed on one another. Drops of water fell off the rim of his hood, streaking down past his stare. A hint of a smile lifted on his lips, catching me off guard.

"You'll find out soon enough." The grim words felt haunted against my skin as he inhaled deeply. "Are you going to take those to him?" He nodded to the flowers in my left hand, and I almost forgot they were there.

I looked down at the petals that were now soaked in water droplets. "Yes."

"Let me take you to him," he demanded, his tone remaining dark and ominous. When my eyebrows slanted downward in confusion, he added, "You can have your time with him. Without me."

His insistence was somewhat comforting, even in the sense that he was only trying to help. But there was a subtle hesitancy, one that kept me on my toes, waiting for a reason.

"I just…" He glanced over his shoulder, scanning the area, before landing back on me. "I just want to make sure you know the way."

With a gentle tilt of my head, I blinked. I don't know how or why, but I could read through his forced sense of security and his words, just like he could mine. I could tell he wasn't giving me the *real* reason—whatever that may be—and I knew that even if I tried, he wouldn't tell me the truth no matter how hard I pressed.

I replied with a simple and flat "sure," and he began walking away from the statue. I followed.

With our steps slow and easy, we walked alongside each other. His stride was long while mine was not, but I still managed to keep his pace. My flowers remained in my left hand while my right hand was shoved in my jacket pocket, keeping dry. We walked in silence for a bit before I turned my head to him.

"Do you always walk in the rain without an umbrella?"

"Do you?" he retaliated.

"No. I mean, I have an umbrella, but I forgot it. But I'm also not the one who is stuck outside constantly, like you."

He shrugged, keeping his gaze ahead. "I don't mind the rain."

"So, you just choose to work here while your clothes are soaking wet?"

Another deep chuckle rattled through his chest as he stole a glance to me. "There are multiple things wrong with that question."

"Okay, such as?"

Before he could answer, his steps stopped. He angled his body toward one of the small stone buildings, causing me to turn and look as well.

It was my Uncle Russ' mausoleum.

Was the walk that short, or was I in my head for most of the way?

The stone looked exactly the same as the last time I was here. Green grass lined the bottom trim, three steps led up to the inside, and a pillar sat on either side of the entrance. Not that I expected anything to be different, but I expected the reality of death to set in more than this.

I wanted time to speed up so I could feel healed, so I could think of him without crying, so I could come here without hurting.

But it was still fresh.

I took one step up the stairs before turning back around. He was still standing there, his hands in his pockets, his jacket still wet, his hood still up.

"Can I ask," I began hesitantly, "what is this place?"

"That's an obscure question."

I fought the urge to roll my eyes at his evasiveness. "The name. What's the name of all this?"

"Does it have to have a name?"

"Don't all cemeteries have names?"

"This isn't a cemetery," he replied, repeating the same statement as before.

"Then what is it?"

He let out a quick, quiet sigh. "You'll see."

I suppressed my groan. "I don't want to see. I want to know," I bit out to him, and he flashed a grin. The move made my core flutter, going against everything my mind was trying to work against.

When it was clear that he wasn't going to give me the information I wanted, I moved the conversation in a different direction. "I have a request."

He gave a nod. "Name it."

"Every Thursday, at three o'clock on the dot, my uncle used to visit me at the coffee shop I work at. I want to do the same for him. I know I have to make appointments or whatever—"

"Done."

I paused, surprised it was that easy. "So, I can come here every Thursday?"

"No, you can come here whenever you want."

My eyes squinted, and my nose slightly scrunched. "But don't I have to schedule something to get in?"

"Celeste Castell," he began, my name echoing through the light sound of the scattered raindrops, "you have twenty-four-seven access to these grounds."

A sarcastic laugh grew in my chest, but I suppressed it down and tilted my head instead. "Just twenty minutes ago, I was almost turned away because I didn't have an appointment. Which is funny, because even if I knew I was required to make one, I wouldn't even know where to begin, because there is no record of this place *anywhere.*"

He exhaled a smooth laugh. "That's the point."

Letting my head roll only a fraction of an inch, I turned myself away from him, refusing to play into his evasiveness any more than I already had. I was here for one reason, and one reason only- to see my uncle on his birthday. I needed to keep that in my mind, rather than focus on the mindfuck that is this cemetery.

Or whatever the hell it is.

"Thank you," I said with my back to him, facing the open entrance to the mausoleum. "I'll be back on Thursday."

And with that, I turned, walked up the remaining steps, and made my way into the open mausoleum. I breathed in the damp, fresh air as I looked around the inside, pulling the hood of my jacket off my head. It was serene and relaxing in here. It was nice.

Approaching the counter that held my uncle's ashes, I eyed the beautiful black matte vase. It was still perfectly centered, and there was no doubt that no one had touched it since it was placed here. I laid the small bouquet of flowers on the surface, letting the petals rest next to the ceramic. I exhaled, feeling a small piece of satisfaction at the sight. If he couldn't be here on Earth, at least he had *this* for his birthday.

But soon, there was a presence at my back, one that I couldn't ignore. It snapped me out of any trance I was lingering in.

"I'll leave you to be with him, I will," his voice rasped. "But let me say one thing."

I turned to face him, only to see he was already up the steps and inside the mausoleum. The rain continued to pour behind him as he walked past the open doorway, blocking any dreary light that was trying to break through. The colored stained-glass windows illuminated his sides, casting a saturated, patterned glow.

He pulled his hood down, and that was the first time I saw all of him.

His hair was dark and rested neatly above his ears. His eyes were a light, piercing grey as they searched mine for any sort of reaction, or any bit of emotion. His cheekbones were high, and his jawbone was sharp, with short, dark stubble lining the bottom half of his face. His hand moved up to his forehead and brushed off any excess water from the rain.

Something in my body leaped at the sight of his hands, his fingers, and the way his motions were fluid and smooth. I tried to keep myself as neutral as possible.

"Those won't do anything."

His voice echoed through the stone walls and rang through my body as I stood there, confused. I said nothing, letting him continue.

"The carnations." He nodded to the flowers on the table.

"Why's that?" I asked, trying my best to push the shake out of my voice.

"Because," he began, his voice doing more to me than it should, "those are the flowers of God. And God isn't here."

As soon as the words left his mouth, he turned to leave, giving me my time with my uncle as promised.

Caius

The monitor that hung on the wall showed no movement. The rain bounced off the leaves, the wind gently pushed the blades of grass, and the iron gates remained closed. I glanced at my watch. It was almost seven, and she had yet to show up.

Leaning back in my chair, I grabbed my glass of whiskey and took a sip. She told me she would be here at exactly three o'clock, so why the delay?

Part of me wanted to get up and get her myself. Actually, every part of me was dying to, just so I could have my sights on her and know that she was safe.

Safe.

Just as much as I wanted her here, I also wanted her as far away from here as possible.

Which is why I kept my eyes glued to the screen ahead, waiting for her white car to roll up the hill.

Finally, a few minutes later, I saw a car on the screen.

But it wasn't white. It was silver.

Fuck.

With a groan, I slammed my glass on the desk and leaned forward in my chair.

I guess today was going to be another one of those days.

With my gaze still on the screen, I watched the security cameras as Lawrence opened the gate for the car, not even bothering to check in. He simply waved, flashed one of his sincere smiles, and closed the gate once the car was through.

As I watched the silver car drive up the pathway to the house, the door to my office burst open, and a flash of blonde hair rushed in.

"Do you want me to kick his ass out of here?" Ace asked, with his fists clenched and his breathing heavy. He must've seen the security feed at the same time I had.

I shook my head slowly. "No, let him say whatever he needs to say. I'm sure it's nothing he hasn't told me already."

Without another word, Ace turned around and left my office, shutting the door behind him. The silence in the room swirled about, leaving my ears ringing, and I knew it was only a matter of seconds before chaos would ensue.

Sure enough, about two minutes later, the door opened. But this time, it wasn't Ace.

It was Amadeus.

It was my fucking *brother.*

"Caius," he said, wasting no time calling to me, his wet, dark hair falling over the crazy, lost look in his eyes. He approached my desk and placed his palms flat on the surface.

Keeping my mouth closed, I simply leaned back in my leather chair and crossed my foot over my knee.

"Caius," he said again, this time sharper. "You *can't* be serious right now."

I rested my elbow on the arm of the chair and waved a hand. "I'm serious."

"You got *another* offer on this place. That doesn't happen often."

He proceeded to speak to me as if I was a toddler who was unable to comprehend the severity of the situation, even though I understood completely.

"And you turned it down?" he asked in verification.

I didn't reply since he clearly already knew my answer.

"For what, Caius? Bragging rights? You turned down an *eight-billion-dollar deal* to gloat?"

A slip of a laugh left my lips as I rubbed my hand against my jaw. "You don't understand, Dey."

"You're right, Cai. I don't. Help me understand, because *I don't.*"

Out of frustration, he pulled his jacket off and tossed it on a nearby chair, sending leftover raindrops flying throughout the room. He pulled the sleeves of his grey shirt up to his elbows, then rested his hands on his hips.

I could practically *feel* his insanity pouring out of him.

"You have the ability to wipe your hands clean of all this. You can get out of here and never come back. Why aren't you leaping at this chance?"

"Because I'm not like you," I said calmly, yet firmly. "I believe in this."

"You believe in playing God?"

A flash of white appeared on the screen over Amadeus' shoulder, forcing my gaze to it. It was a white car.

Her car.

"Fuck," I muttered under my breath and quickly stood to my feet. Amadeus followed my gaze and turned to look at the screen, his vision briefly catching on the white car as well. She stopped and rolled her window down a few inches, and Lawrence made his way to her with a warm greeting. She only sat there for a few seconds before Lawrence let her through the open gates.

"Who is that?" he asked, his eyebrows cinching downward.

Her car rolled in and pulled off to the side, and my eyes stayed glued to it the entire time.

"You need to leave," I replied as I reached for my black rain jacket and put it on.

Amadeus ignored my demand as he remained still in my office, his gaze locked on the screen. "Is that the person that made you the offer?"

"No."

"What is it up to now, offer number three?" he asked.

I shook my head. "Offer four. Now *go.*"

Without waiting to see if he would actually leave, I headed out and shut the door to my office. After walking down the window-lined hall and into the main corridor, I pushed open the front door and jogged down the steps, not bothering to pull up my hood. Rain instantly drenched my dark hair, but I couldn't care less.

Because there she was.

She was walking down the path without an umbrella, her jeans growing dark from the heavy raindrops, her black jacket zipped all the way up her chest. She was nearing her uncle's mausoleum. With a few quick strides, I caught up to her and quietly approached her back. I could see strands of her dark brown hair poking out from the sides of her hood, becoming wavy in the deep humidity.

And here I was, drawn to her like a fucking magnet, my body reacting to her in ways it never did with anyone else.

I watched as she stood at the bottom of the steps, too wary to enter.

I know that stance, that hesitancy. I've seen it hundreds of times.

Her grief was growing heavier, not becoming easier.

"It's after seven," I cut through the natural silence and spoke with a darkness that couldn't be lightened.

She jumped slightly but tried to cover the movement. Her head turned to look at me over her shoulder, pausing as she caught sight of my rain-soaked face. "Oh, I'm sorry, I know I said I'd be here, but they needed me to cover a shift at the coffee shop."

I raised a hand. "No need to apologize, Celeste. You can come here whenever you'd like…"

The last word trailed off my tongue, lingering in the empty space between us. She took notice and completely turned to face me, her sparkling honey-colored eyes catching my gaze.

I continued. "…but it's almost sundown."

She instantly nodded. "I know, I know. Cemeteries close at dusk."

I blinked. She knew what she was doing, and she was doing it so fucking well. She was purposely looking for me to correct her so she could use it as an invitation for information.

And I was more than happy to play her game.

"This isn't a cemetery."

"Are you ever going to tell me what it is, then? Is it some sacred burial grounds? An underground morgue? A death cult?"

Ah, she's a smartass. I like that.

I couldn't help the small smirk that rose on my lips. "I guess it's a little bit of all of those. But, if you want it to be a cult, then it's a cult."

She rolled her eyes, and instead of fighting me back, instead of rattling off some sarcastic remark, she turned her back to me and walked up the steps of the mausoleum.

Within seconds, the sound of a car came up to my back, driving past me on the path. Rain beat on the windshield, and the wipers moved to push it away. I turned to look, even though I already knew who it was.

"You know we're not done talking about this, Caius," Amadeus said through his open window.

Out of the corner of my eye, I saw movement in the open doorframe of the mausoleum, and I knew Celeste was listening. She moved closer, waiting for more to be said.

"I know," I replied hastily, not wanting to say anything else in front of Celeste.

But it was too late, because Amadeus caught a glimpse of her, and it was game over.

He nodded in her direction but continued to speak to me. "Is she staying for the show?" he asked with a smug-ass grin on his face, and Celeste's vision volleyed from him to me.

My stare turned deadly as I shot a look to Amadeus. "Go."

His smile never faded as he rolled up his window and drove off, leaving me to deal with the repercussions of his words.

"Show?" Celeste inquired. I looked back to her, only to see her delicate head tilted to the side.

Fuck, I didn't want to do this, at least not yet. I knew it was going to happen at some point, just by the way she consumed my thoughts already, but I was hoping to wait until her grief had faded a bit. A big part of me was numb to other people's feelings and didn't care much about emotions, but I wasn't a complete monster. It hadn't even been a *month* since her uncle passed, and now she was about to have her entire world ripped apart and turned upside down.

When it rains, it pours.

"What does that mean?" she continued, slowly making her way back down the steps. Locks of her hair gently framed her face as she descended, and her gaze lit up with curiosity. I forced myself to watch her eyes the whole way, not giving her any reaction as her body neared mine, even though my lower half couldn't help but answer to her presence. Mentally, I tried to get my stiffening cock to settle the fuck down, but it had a mind of its own.

When her foot hit the bottom, she lifted her chin up to me, careful to not let the hood of her jacket slide off her head.

And I looked down at her, my jaw tight and my shoulders square.

Only a select group of people knew what this place *really* was, and *none* of them were any of the women I'd pursued in the past. I've always kicked them out before sundown, and none of them were curious enough to ask why. And I sure as fuck never cared enough about them to let them in on the secret.

Until *now.*

Until *her.*

It was only a matter of time before she knew.

There was something about her that made me want to let her in. There was a mystery to *her* that settled in well to the mystery of all *this.* And I wasn't going to let it go anytime soon.

She blinked up at me, her dark eyelashes fluttering against the soft skin of her cheeks. *"Caius,"* she said, tasting the nectar of my name on her tongue, letting the sound roll off her lips for the very first time.

And that was the moment I could feel the deepest parts of me shatter.

She knew me, she knew my name. She *had* me.

It was that simple.

"You need to come with me," I rasped, breaking eye contact with her and turning away. I began to walk down the path and waited for her to follow.

Celeste

Puddles of water splashed under my feet as I jogged to catch up. Caius was only a few steps ahead, but his strides were so long that reaching him took me longer than expected.

"Caius," I prodded, and I could see his muscles tense at the sound of his name coming from my lips. "Who was that? And what was he talking about?"

Caius ignored me and kept walking. The rain from above began to taper off as the sky darkened with nightfall. I glanced upward to see the rain clouds slowly being replaced with darkness. Keeping my hand on my hood, I shielded myself from the leftover drops.

"Caius," I pleaded again. There was an urgency in his voice earlier, one that I couldn't shake. I didn't want to go with him, despite my curiosity, but the aching seriousness in his voice was real.

Very real.

"Just come with me," he commanded, neither one of us breaking stride. His hood remained down, and streams of water dripped off his dark hair and down his smooth neck.

He led me to a house, one that was larger than I could've ever expected to be on a plot of land like this. The entire home was painted black, from roof to ground. The tall roof came to several rounded points, almost looking like a modern cathedral. On the right side of the structure was a long corridor of floor-to-ceiling glass that allowed me to see inside perfectly. Lingering rainwater ran down the windows, creating a soft, streaked illusion, with dim lighting filtering out from the inside. It was gorgeous and beautifully made, and I gasped at the sight.

Caius guided me to the front steps, and as he stepped up the first few, I remained at the bottom. He must've felt the lack of presence behind him because he paused to turn around.

"Celeste," he began, releasing a soft plea in his voice. Suddenly, I knew this entire situation was bigger than me, bigger than my heart's reach, bigger than my understanding.

I pulled my arms up to my chest. "Is this… your house?"

"Yes."

"Do you live here?"

He smirked. "Yes."

"Do you…" My voice trailed off as I tried to piece the facts together. "You don't just work here, do you?"

He shook his head. "Not by a long shot." Before I could ask anything more, and with his body slowly turning back to the front door, he spared me one last glance as he cocked his head in the direction of the house. "Come in."

Hesitancy filled my every pore as I followed him up the stairs and inside. Caius led me down the glass corridor, stopping halfway down the hall. He turned and faced the window, and I mirrored his actions as I stood to his right. The outside rain was now a fine mist as the rest of the gloomy daylight faded. I pulled my hood off my head, exposing my dark brown hair in a loose—now wavy—braid. I pulled it over my shoulder, then placed my hands back in my jacket pockets.

I could feel Caius look at me from the corner of his eye. He was trying not to stare, but I could feel the heat of it. My chest felt heavy at his attention, and my lungs tightened at the thought of him letting me in.

He was opening the door to his world to me.

A few long, drawn-out moments of silence surrounded us before I got the courage to speak again.

"What did he mean back there? What's this 'show' he mentioned?"

He didn't answer. Instead, he used his hand to shake his dark hair of any excess rainwater.

He kept his gaze on the land ahead, the area riddled with a handful of pathways and hundreds of beautifully built mausoleums. His face was stoic as I continued to watch him, waiting for him to give me *any* sort of clue of what was to come.

Finally, the clouded sun had officially set, and his body turned tense. Even more tense than it already was.

"Celeste," he turned to face me, his hand reaching to grab my arm. "I need you to listen to me very carefully. What I'm about to tell you—what I'm about to *show you*—is real, and I need you to stay with me, okay?"

Oh, shit. My heart thumped at his drastic, dark words. *What have I gotten myself into?*

I swallowed the newly formed lump in my throat as I nodded.

With his eyes still on mine, Caius squinted and his eyebrows furrowed, a sudden confusion striking his face. The hand that was clutching my arm moved up to the left side of my face, where I felt a drop of rainwater slide down my cheek.

"What is this?" he asked, his thumb brushing away the water.

Because I was so caught up in whatever was about to happen, it took me a moment to realize what he was confused about. My makeup was beginning to come off. I quickly took a step back and swatted his hand away, moving my own up to cover my cheek.

"Nothing, it's nothing."

His jaw ticked, and his head tilted at my lie. Panic began to set in as I kept my hand on the left side of my face. Sure, he was letting me into whatever *this* was, but I wasn't ready to let him into my side of secrets. At least, not yet.

Just as I was about to fabricate some stupid lie, I saw a quick movement out of the corner of my eye. There was something outside, and I turned my head to look.

The rain had stopped completely. There was a woman walking across the dark path in front of the window. She was dressed in an all-black dress, the bottom hem gliding along the stone with each soft step she took. She didn't bother to look at us as she continued on.

"I thought you guys closed at night? What is she doing here?"

Caius watched her out the window, a small grin forming on his lips.

A man came from the other direction, walking down the same path in front of the window, not sparing us a glance either. He passed the woman in black without greeting and made his way out of sight.

"Are you gonna go tell them to leave?" I asked with my palm still resting on my face.

Caius shook his head, the smirk still there. "No."

"You gave them twenty-four-hour access, too?" I asked, still confused as to what this all meant. I didn't know why I was in here, why he was showing me this, and why I needed to know in the first place.

"Not technically," he began, then took a deep breath. He turned back to me, eyeing the hand still covering my face. He shook his head, and I knew he was saving his comments to address it later.

"Nighttime is special here, Celeste. Nighttime is when there's nowhere to hide, no matter how hard you try. Darkness might shield you, but it never erases who you are."

I narrowed my eyes at him, my mind lost in his riddled words.

"Those people you see, wandering the paths, they aren't here."

My heartbeat sped up at his implication.

"They were once *here,* of this world, but they're not anymore."

My mouth became dry as I tried to swallow the information, but I couldn't. Another person walked by. It was a young man, probably in his late thirties. He wore a button-up shirt with a vest over top and a beret on his head. He looked very old-fashioned, and suddenly the severity of this situation grew extremely heavy on my shoulders.

"They are ghosts."

My hand dropped from my face as I stared out the window. More and more of them appeared, all of them walking aimlessly around the land as night set in. They wove between each other, not paying each other any mind, each person on their own way.

"And this, Celeste," his voice darkened, his tone haunting as it rattled the marrow of my bones. I could feel his intense stare on me, but I couldn't bring myself to tear my eyes away from the sight outside. "This is Purgatory."

Glass shattered

Burn every paper

Red water

Before I knew it, my legs were carrying me out of that house faster than I could process it. I ran to the front door, flung it open, and ran down the front steps.

Normally, I'd avoid running straight into my fears, but I had to get out of there. I needed to get to my car.

My breath was caught in my throat as my feet found the stone path, at least a dozen ghosts surrounding me. I did my best to steer clear of them all, my vision circling every bit of land I could see, my body turning in odd ways to prevent myself from bumping into them.

I wasn't even sure if I *could* touch them.

"Celeste!" I heard a voice call out to my back. I ignored it and pressed on, weaving through mausoleums and statues and *ghosts.*

After finally making it to my car, I got inside and turned it on. As the engine roared, the headlights flicked on, illuminating the view in front of me.

My eyes widened as my heart fell into my ass.

The ghosts were brightened to their highest opacity, forcing my aching pupils to dilate. They were bright, brighter than I'd ever seen, but even the shine of the lights didn't faze them. They continued to walk the paths, their souls in everlasting limbo as they meandered slowly. You would think the light would go straight through them since they weren't physical beings, but it didn't. It reflected. They had an eternal glow to them, one that couldn't be seen in the dark. Their everlasting haze burned into my vision, leaving their bright imprint beneath my eyelids.

And that's when I knew this picture would be seared in my memory forever.

Turning my car around, I tried to dodge my way through the ghosts. I made it to the entrance, and the man working the booth opened the gates, allowing my car through.

I didn't hesitate to push my foot to the pedal.

But as the gates closed behind me and my car began its descent down the winding hill, I took one last look in the rearview mirror. The ghosts were still strolling as if there wasn't a care in their world.

Maybe that was it. Maybe they didn't care.

Because they couldn't.

A week has gone by since the night at the cemetery.

This isn't a cemetery.

I squeezed my eyes shut, pushing his words from my head. He was right—it *wasn't* a cemetery—but in his truth, I wasn't expecting *this*.

Did I even believe it? Was it all true?

For the past seven nights, I had a reoccurring nightmare about the ghosts. I was back there, it was nighttime, and I was running to my car. But once I was there, I couldn't get in. The doors were locked, and no matter how hard I tried to pull on the handle, it never opened. The ghosts surrounded me, stared at me, and made it known that they knew I existed. They wanted me. They reached for me. Through all that, Caius was nowhere to be found, with no desire to save me from my fears.

Then, I would wake up in a cold sweat, with my breathing heavy and my heart racing. And most of the time, I had no chance of falling back to sleep.

Now, it was Thursday again, and I wasn't sure if I could bring myself to drive back to that place. I didn't want to put myself in a position of vulnerability when I was already so vulnerable. The loss of my uncle still had a sting that wasn't ready to heal, and I didn't want to add a fresh fear to the mix.

But when I thought about Uncle Russ and who he was as a person, that's when things *really* started to get confusing.

Why did he choose to rest there? What were his reasons?

How did he even find out about it?

And why didn't I see his ghost that night?

Maybe it was the fact that I hauled ass out of there faster than I could look at the faces of the ghosts.

In my car, I sat in the parking lot of the coffee shop. My shift ended twenty minutes ago, but I couldn't bring myself to leave. I didn't want to go home, but I wasn't sure if I was ready to go back to the…

This isn't a cemetery.

Pressing the heels of my palms to my eyes, I rubbed them until I saw stars. I needed to get his fucking voice out of my fucking head before I started screaming.

Despite my internal dismay telling me to not go back, the grief for my uncle outweighed my fear. I wanted to visit him, I wanted to see him every Thursday like he did for me.

And if I go during the day, avoiding nightfall at all costs, I'll be fine.

Pulling out of the parking lot, I made my way toward the unknowns of my state. It was about a forty-minute drive from the coffee shop, putting me at my uncle's mausoleum right at three o'clock.

Taking the back roads, heavy forestry and thick woods lined both sides of the pavement, guiding me in a drive that was quiet and peaceful. There were hardly any cars on the road with me. I turned up my radio and put on my playlist, letting the music calm any nerves that were trying to bubble their way up to the surface.

Then, with about five minutes left of the drive, my music cut out. While carefully keeping my eyes on the road, I picked up my phone and brought it to eye level. All service was gone, and a bright "SOS" signal appeared in the corner.

Great. At least I know I'm close.

I turned into the hidden driveway, the one I've turned into a handful of times already. There was a deep fog coating the roads as raindrops began to cover my windshield. I turned on my wipers, but it didn't seem to help much as I made my way up the hill.

After familiar twists and turns, my car found the iron gates. I cracked my window down an inch as the same older man came out of his booth.

"Good afternoon, Miss Castell. It's good to see you again," he smiled cheerfully. "Can I get you anything?"

I could feel my face return the happy expression. His joy was contagious, and it momentarily erased my anxiety.

"No, I think I'm okay, thank you."

"Well, you let me know if there's anything you need."

With a nod, he went back into his booth and opened the gates. My car slowly rolled through the remainder of the fog, and I parked off to the side. Thankfully, I remembered my umbrella this time. I grabbed it from the backseat and opened it as soon as I stepped out. Heavy rain pelted the fabric, the drops turning to liquid beads and rolling off.

I wanted to see my uncle and avoid Caius at all costs, despite the comfort he brings to me when I'm here.

Maybe it was the fact that he had all the answers to any question I might have. He held a sense of security in his information. Knowledge is power, yes, but knowledge also forms peace of mind.

Without moving my head, I quickly glanced around the area. There was no one else here. Everything seemed peaceful and serene, and it was hard for me to imagine all the ghosts that wandered the paths the last time I was here.

But when I blinked, a flash of memory sparked through me, and the image of that night sent a quick shiver through my body.

They were here, they were *all here*, but it was daytime.

Were they hiding, waiting, or resting?

Did they know I was here?

I quickly shook my head and began walking. I could think about all this later, once I was gone.

I walked on the stone path in the direction of my uncle's mausoleum. It was a short walk, and now that I've been here a few times, I could mindlessly find it without paying attention.

I approached the front of the structure, and my vision eyed the *Castell* etched in the top stone.

"Hi, Uncle Russ," I whispered. After closing and dropping my umbrella, I stepped up into the open mausoleum. It was still clean, still polished, and still beautiful. I walked to one of the benches along the side and sat down.

My eyes were glued to the black vase that was neatly presented on the island.

"What are you doing here?" I quietly asked the ceramic container. "Why here?"

There was a deafening pause as I deeply inhaled.

"There *has* to be a reason why you chose this place," I continued, talking more to myself than to his ashes. "If what Caius says is true, then there *has* to be a reason why you would want to rest here."

I could hear and feel the lump in my throat grow, the ache turning more uncomfortable with each passing moment. I thought about all the times Uncle Russ played with me as a kid; all the times he pushed me on the swings, the times he would color in my coloring books with me, and even the times when he would build sandcastles with me and Serena at the beach.

I can't see a man like *that* wanting to rest in a place like *this*. Don't we all want the sun on our skin, rather than the rain in our hair?

No matter how beautiful it is here, its underlying truth isn't an ideal destination.

I instantly sat up as a thought struck me. *Truth.*

Who said Caius was telling the truth?

Maybe he was bullshitting me. Maybe he was trying to get a rise out of me, scare me off, or even just play a stupid joke on me. Maybe he was trying to get me to never come back here. He was doing well keeping this place a secret and completely under wraps, and he didn't want a girl like me to ruin that.

Or, maybe he was confused. Maybe he thinks this place is Purgatory, but in reality, it's just a graveyard.

It's just a cemetery.

A small laugh escaped me as I moved to stand up. Any fear I had up until this point left my body, and I was able to convince myself that all I had left was lingering grief.

"I'll see you next week, Uncle Russ."

My fingers brushed against the smooth countertop as I said a silent goodbye. As soon as I walked out of the open doorframe, I stopped.

There he was. *Caius.*

"How long have you been there?" I asked.

"Not long," he assured. "I wanted to give you your privacy."

He stood at the bottom of the steps with his jacket on, hood up, and hands in his pockets. I watched his bright eyes through the rainfall, the strips of water clouding my vision.

"Privacy, right," I nodded. I grabbed my umbrella and walked down the steps. "Is this how you give privacy to everyone who comes to your cemetery?"

The tone of my question was warm, but there was a hint of sarcasm in the last word. *Cemetery.*

His eyes locked with mine as I walked off the last step, opened the umbrella, and stood in front of him. I could feel his body heat through his clothes, radiating onto me, even though there were layers of fabric between us.

As he clenched his jaw and furrowed his brows, his voice hovered above a deep whisper. "You don't believe me."

I gave a sympathetic smirk. "I don't."

"Even though you saw it all with your own eyes?"

I shrugged. "Guess not."

"Why?"

I could see a hint of heartache in his eyes, but I did my best to ignore it.

After a brief pause, I exhaled. "Because, Caius," I started, and his facial expression softened at the sound of his name. The sight of him giving in to me, even only by a fraction, had me momentarily faltering. "It doesn't make any sense. There's no way this can be real."

His eyes trailed down to my lips, watching me speak before moving back to my eyes. With a pinch of hesitancy, he turned his head to look down the path, away from both the entrance and my car. He waited a moment before turning back to me, a new confidence in his expression.

"Would you give me one final chance to prove to you that it's real?" he asked, the sound of a plea buried under the layers of his voice.

Studying him, I tilted my head. As he waited for my answer, a handful of thoughts were speeding around my head, jumbling any reasoning that was trying to break through the noise.

"Why me?" I began. "Why are you trying so hard to convince *me?*"

His face hardened at my question, and his body turned stiff as he kept his eyes on me. My umbrella hovered over both my head and the space between us, allowing us to keep our gazes locked without anything between us.

I'd be lying if I said I wasn't intrigued.

I'd *also* be lying if I said I didn't like the way he was restless for my approval.

But for what? Why did he want my validation? Why did he want me to see what he saw?

"Don't deflect. Answer me, Celeste." His hand moved under my chin, his warm fingers pushing to lift my gaze higher.

The simple gesture of his touch electrified me, lighting up something in me that could not be dimmed.

"Will you give me one last chance to prove to you that this is real?"

With his hand still under my chin and his thumb gently resting along the curve of my jaw, words refused to find their way out of me. My throat was constricted with a newly formed need, a craving for something in the unknown. I did my best to nod in response.

He dropped his hand back to his side, his skin taking the electric current with it. "Saturday. Be here at four. Drive up to the house."

Without any explanation, he turned and walked off in the other direction. Raindrops streamed down the hood and shoulders of his jacket, dripping off of him in small splashes, and he continued on as if he was completely immune to the natural downpour. Before I could form a cohesive thought, before I could ask for more information, he was gone.

"Hey, are you busy?" I asked, with the phone pressed to my ear and my hand on the steering wheel.

"No, why?"

"Because I'm in your driveway."

Silence stilled on the other end of the line. Faintly, I could hear footsteps trot across the floor and rustling soon after. I looked up, and sure enough, Serena pulled open her front curtain to look at me from the window.

"What are you doing here?" she asked.

"I want to show you something. Bring Nolan. We can drop him off at Mom's on the way."

I could sense Serena's hesitation over the phone, and a deep sigh accompanied it.

"I promise we won't be long."

"Fine. Give me a minute."

The call clicked off, and I dropped my phone in my lap.

Yesterday, after Caius invited me back on Saturday for *who-knows-what*, I spent the entire night thinking about it. Imagining it. Molding the idea of it in my head like putty. When I showered, I tried to figure out what it was that he was inviting me to. What was he trying to show me? His directions were too specific for it to simply be just another conversation. Were other people going to be involved this time? Was the other guy going to be there, the one who asked if I was staying for *"the show"* and indirectly started this whole thing?

Was there going to be another show?

Then, when I laid in bed, I kept denying the thought of Purgatory as a whole. There is no way it was only a short drive away from my house, in the high hills of the countryside, hidden away but still findable. In the whole face of the Earth, *that's* where Purgatory is? *That's* where people's answers lie? And somehow, it has managed to stay a secret this whole time? It just didn't make sense, and therefore, it couldn't be true.

And finally, when I dreamt, I pictured my uncle, satisfied with where he was resting. Even in the doom and gloom, he was content with his choices. He was happy.

But then I woke up and knew my mind had to be playing games with me.

This whole situation felt like one giant puzzle that I needed to fix. Or destroy. Or ignore altogether.

A few minutes later, Serena came out of her house with her arms full. She held Nolan in one elbow, his smile as happy as can be, and his car seat and diaper bag in the other. I quickly hopped out of the car and reached for Nolan, who reached for me back.

"This better be good. Nolan was happily napping when you called."

Nolan squealed in excitement as I bounced him up and down in my arms. "He seems to still be happy."

Serena hooked up the car seat in the backseat and replied, "Yeah, give it an hour. He'll be cranky again."

"I'm sure Mom will have no problem with him."

With Nolan safely buckled in, we all drove to my parents' house. My mom was more than happy to watch Nolan, and when we dropped him off, he was still his smiley self as he chewed on his rubber teething toy. When we got back in the car and began to drive away, that's when Serena started asking her questions.

"Where are we going?"

"To see Uncle Russ."

"Oh. Okay. I've been wanting to see where he's buried, but why? Why now?"

With a subtle shake of my head, I tried to remain vague without giving too much away. "I just thought you could go with me this time."

"This time? Do you do this frequently?"

"No," I said in a half truth. I *don't* visit frequently, but in her question, I realized that I've been there more often than most people. "I was referring to the burial service," I added, swallowing my lie.

Serena accepted my answer, and we continued to talk as the drive went on, mainly about the memories we had with Uncle Russ. I could tell Serena was beginning to get emotional, which I had expected since this was her first time visiting him.

And hopefully, we'll have no problem getting through the gates.

When we got close, Serena's phone lost all service. "What the fuck?" she asked, turning the screen of her phone to show me the lack of signal.

"Yeah, it does that here."

Her eyebrows furrowed in confusion.

"It's just a dead zone, I guess," I added.

We turned onto the winding road. Fog covered every inch of visibility as I followed the curved path. Serena leaned forward, squinting her eyes as she tried to see *anything.*

"How can you see where you're going?"

"I can't, really."

The rain began in small taps on the windshield, growing heavier as I continued on.

"Holy shit, Cel. This is creepy."

I nodded in response as we finally made it up the hill. The dense fog broke, and we drove up to the gates. The man at the booth took one look at my car, gave me a quick wave, and shouted over the rainfall.

"Good afternoon, Miss Castell!"

I smiled and waved back from my window, hoping he was able to see my greeting through the streaks of rain.

"He knows you?" Serena nudged my arm, and I gave a slow nod. A sudden guilt struck me at the realization that he knew me and my name, but I didn't know his.

My response was slow as I watched him out my window. "He must remember me from the service."

It was an obvious lie, but I said it partially in protection, and partially in denial. I didn't want her to know about Caius, and I didn't want her to know what all this really was.

Not yet.

I pulled the car through the open gates and parked off to the side. Grabbing the umbrella from the back seat, I hopped out of the car, and Serena did the same.

"I didn't think it was supposed to rain today," she said to me as I opened the umbrella and held it above us. It barely managed to cover us both as long as we squeezed together and leaned in. I shrugged in response, brushing away the remark.

There's a lot she doesn't know.

As I led the way to the mausoleum, Serena glanced around. "This place is beautiful."

"Yeah, it is," I echoed. I don't know if it was because of the rain, but the leaves seemed to look extra green today. The trees soaked in the excess water, the moss collected the drops, and everything looked more than healthy.

Maybe it was because I was looking through the eyes of Serena, someone who was seeing all this for the first time. The shimmer of the novelty was there.

But maybe, if she finds out that *this*—according to Caius— is actually the realm between Heaven and Hell, she won't see it as beautiful anymore.

Then again, is it fair to this place to not be considered beautiful just because of the label it wears?

As we were walking, heavy footsteps came from the path to our left, releasing me from my train of thought. A hooded man walked toward us, and I prayed that it wasn't Caius. I didn't need my sister meeting him.

Not yet.

But as soon as I turned to look, I could tell it wasn't him. This man had a similar body type, with a towering height and broad shoulders, but I could see the difference in the way he carried himself. He seemed more…friendly.

Before I knew it, he was right in front of us.

"Compliments of the Estates."

His voice was smooth as he extended his arm to Serena and held out a brand-new umbrella. I watched as Serena's eyes met his, their gazes connected, a powerful and surging moment in time. Without looking away, she slowly took the umbrella and muttered a quiet "Thank you."

The man gave a single nod and briefly glanced to me. I smirked in return as he shifted on his feet and walked back the way he came.

"Holy shit," Serena whispered to me as she opened the umbrella, and I couldn't help but smile. Based on the rosy blush on her cheeks, I knew exactly what she was thinking, and I didn't blame her one bit. Whoever he may be, he was intriguing and enigmatic, to say the least.

With each of us under our own umbrella, we continued the short walk to the mausoleum. I stopped in front of the structure and looked up, and Serena did the same.

Even though I was still sad and grieving, this was a totally different experience for Serena. This was the first time visiting him and seeing his resting place, and it was only the beginning of her life without him.

I heard her sharp inhale at the sight of our last name on the top of the building.

I looked at her and nodded to the entrance. "Go ahead. I can wait out here."

Serena hesitated, her eyes still glued to the cursive name etched in the stone. "Will you go with me?" she asked, and I could hear the quiver in her voice. Meanwhile, there was no hesitation in mine.

"Of course."

Looping my arm in hers, we both ascended the steps and closed our umbrellas. Once inside, Serena looked around to the beautiful, perfectly kept inside. I moved to sit on the stone bench along the wall while Serena approached the ceramic urn. She motioned to it and looked at me, as if questioning if that was it.

I nodded, and she looked back to the vase.

And she cried.

Tears slid down her cheeks freely, her emotions coming in waves as she let go. Her feelings rushed to the surface as she held her face in her hands, her shoulders heaving with sorrow.

I felt that, too.

I felt it all before Caius revealed all the secrets to me. Now, I don't know what I feel.

Serena sat down on the bench across from me and wiped the tears away with the back of her hands. "God, this sucks."

I crossed my arms over my chest. "I know."

More tears cascaded down her face, but they began to slow. Her rivers of tears decreased to a few drops a minute, then lessened again to a heavy glisten lining her bottom lids. I looked over to the urn, my expression blank as I seared the image of it into my mind.

"At least he's here," Serena spoke. "It seems like a nice place to be."

Looking back at her, I stared at her sad expression as she tried to find the silver lining.

But there wasn't one.

"Yeah," was all I managed to force out, and my attempt at covering my tone in a fake sincerity failed.

Serena caught on instantly. "What?"

"Nothing."

Serena's sadness switched to confusion. "No, what? Why are you mad?"

"I'm not."

"Yes, you are," Serena pushed. "It's obvious. It's written all over you."

I thought about what she was referring to. Maybe it was the fact that my arms were still tightly crossed over my chest, or maybe it was the fact that I caught myself giving a soft scowl with narrowed eyes. Probably both.

"I'm fine," I said, uncrossing my arms and easing my expression. "I just… I think he deserves better."

"Better?" Serena asked, shocked. "Cel, this place is beautiful. He must've loved it if he chose it."

Words stuck in my throat, and I remained quiet.

"I think it's perfect. I feel like… if I had to pick somewhere for myself, I'd choose this, too. What do you mean *better?"*

He chose it. I'd choose this. Her words were like a sharp stabbing in my ears.

"Nothing, Serena. Stop."

Serena straightened herself and took the hint. We both looked away from one another, and I immediately felt bad for snapping at her. The thought of telling her what I know appeared once again. I could fill her in on the supposed "truth" to this, but since I myself didn't know if it was true, I decided to keep it to myself.

After a few more minutes of silence between us and the white noise of the rain around us, Serena stood up. "Let's go," she demanded, clearly still hurt and not trying to hide it.

We grabbed our umbrellas, opened them, and made our way back to my car. Before getting in, I took one final look around. Caius was nowhere to be seen.

Celeste

The iron gates were open and welcoming to me as my car rolled up the hill. Saturday, Four o'clock, right on time. The older man from the booth raised his hand in a wave, greeting me in his usual chipper tone. "Good afternoon, Miss Castell!" I heard his muffled shout through the rain on my window.

My eyebrows creased at the sight of the man's clothes. He was wearing suit pants, a dress shirt, and a fitted suit jacket. An umbrella rested over his shoulder, shielding him from the standard rainfall as he held a clipboard in his free hand. Of all the times I've been here, he's never looked this sharp and presentable before. Not even for my uncle's burial.

I stored the thought away as I rolled down my window halfway, avoiding the pelts of rain slipping through. "Excuse me!" I shouted to him, and he smiled. "I never got your name."

"Lawrence," he replied, with a polite grin and tip of his chin.

"Nice to meet you, *again,* Lawrence."

His smile widened as he gestured me through. "Enjoy your visit!"

I continued driving, pulling past the usual place I park my car to drive up toward the house. The beautiful, tall home greeted me with rich, green landscaping and warm lighting spilling out from within. I made my way up to the front of the house, where a young man waited under a makeshift awning. With his hood pulled over his head, he jogged to my window, and I proceeded to roll it down.

"Keys?" he asked, squinting as he blinked away a few raindrops.

"What?"

"This is a valet," he stated. "Keys?" he asked again, this time with his hand stretched out.

I didn't want to keep him in the rain, so I opened the door, stepped out, and handed him my keys. Within seconds, he pulled my car out of sight and around the house.

Valet? Why was there a valet service here? And why was Lawrence dressed so nicely?

With my hood over my head, I trotted up the front steps of the house, and before I could reach for the doorbell, the front door swung open.

"Come in," a hand reached out, the palm stretching past me and gently resting on the back of my shoulder. It was an offer to guide me indoors and to get me out of the rain. I stepped inside, swiped my hood down, and looked at the person who let me in.

"Celeste?" he asked, as if he was making sure I was who he thought I was.

I nodded.

I knew him.

He seemed so familiar, with his blonde hair falling in waves over his bright green eyes, and his broad shoulders framing his muscular body. He was recognizable in the sense that I'd seen him before, but something was different.

"Compliments of the Estates."

He was the one who gave me the umbrella on the day of my uncle's burial.

He was the one who gave Serena her umbrella only yesterday.

He no longer wore a heavy raincoat. There was no hood hiding him. There was no rain blurring the image of him.

I blinked up at him, and he gave me a slight smirk. He knew I remembered.

"I'm Ace," he said, extending his hand. I placed my small palm in his, and he gave a polite squeeze. "May I show you around?"

My eyes moved away from him to look at the inside of the house. I was already in here once before, but because Caius and I had other things to talk about, I never had the chance to study the inside.

Before we stepped away from the front door, I quickly glanced down the hallway where we stood last week, where he took me to watch the ghosts for the first time. I stared at the spot where we once stood, where I saw a sight that changed something in me forever.

Whether I believed in it or not.

Ace led me to the bottom of the grand staircase, which was only a few steps inside the front corridor. It led up to a giant curved window that covered the entire wall, where the steps then split into opposite directions. My eyes followed the path as we went up the left set of stairs, the rain continuing to tap softly against the glass next to me.

Ace pointed out every door along our walk as he led me down the hall. There were a few guest bedrooms, more than enough bathrooms, and even a small library. The walls were a deep, dark green, with dim, warm lighting every few steps. It was cozy, it was comforting, and I found myself in awe of the simplicity of the home.

"And this," Ace began, reaching for the handle of the last door, "is for you."

My gaze locked on Ace as he smirked, flashing a brief yet sincere grin. His demeanor helped me feel surprisingly calm, and his body language showed nothing but authenticity.

He pushed open the door and allowed me through first.

It was a large, open bedroom. Lit candles were scattered around, sitting in corners and flickering on the surfaces of the dresser and end tables, lifting the room in a sweet aroma. There was a set of large, glass balcony doors along one side of the room, while a king-sized bed rested against the adjacent wall. Across the length of the bed was a white silk dress, the fabric flawless and perfectly seamless. It had thin straps, a scoop neckline, and a high hem in the front that flowed into a lower hem in the back.

My mouth fell open at the sight of the beautiful dress, and I reluctantly looked at Ace.

"What? What is…"

He gave a knowing smirk, not bothering to explain.

"Hi!" A high-pitched voice popped in, and I jumped at the sound.

It was a woman, maybe a few years older than me, standing on the other side of Ace. Had she been here the whole time?

Her smile beamed at me. She was tall, like Ace, and had the same blonde hair as him. In fact, she had the same striking green eyes, golden skin, and soft facial features as him as well. My eyes caught the shimmer of a gold necklace resting below her collarbones, with the letters M. A. dangling in the middle.

"My name is Melanie-Aurora, but that's a mouthful. Just call me Mel." She passed Ace and wrapped her arms around me, giving me a tight hug. Even though I was still confused and definitely caught off guard, I returned the gesture and gently hugged her back.

Ace slowly stepped to the door. "I'll leave you to it," he nodded, then started to close the door behind him.

"To what?" I asked, but he clicked the door shut.

Mel turned to me, the wide smile still spread on her face.

"Are you ready?" she asked playfully. There was clearly more to this setup than I expected.

"For…"

"For tonight."

Without waiting for a reply, Mel took my hand and led me to a door that was on the other side of the room.

She pushed it open, and I gasped at the sight.

The flames of more candles flickered as we stepped inside this master bathroom. To the left, there was a white porcelain countertop with a sink in the middle and a circular mirror above it. Green vines hung along the wall, accenting the glass and wrapping its way down the side of the cabinetry. To the right was a walk-in shower, one that looked large enough to belong in its own room. There were multiple showerheads along the walls and a waterfall nozzle on the ceiling. More plants lined the inside of the shower, creating a natural and organic intensity. Next to the clear shower doors, fresh, clean towels sat in a basket, and a black robe hung on a hook above it.

But then, as my vision moved forward, I found the most beautiful part of the bathroom.

A large, white, clawfoot tub rested on the farthest side of the bathroom. Next to it was a floor-to-ceiling window, one that arched at the top with an intricate Victorian design. There were black steel beams that ran from top to bottom, elongating the appearance of the glass. Rain pattered the window, as it always does here, but it brought a soft, soothing ambiance to the room that couldn't be matched.

A piece of me was begging for Mel to tell me to soak in the tub, Caius and ghosts be damned.

But she didn't.

"Celeste?" she asked, snapping me out of my stare.

"Sorry," I shook my head. "It's just… I think this is the nicest bathroom I've ever been in."

Mel nodded. "Same here. It's nicer than mine down the hall. I'm surprised Cai let us use it for the night."

My head snapped to the side, my eyes wide with shock. "What? This is *his* bathroom?"

Mel nodded with a subtle grin on her lips, but it wasn't subtle enough to hide what she was *really* thinking.

He was letting me in, in *every* aspect of this place. Including his personal space.

But why?

"Do you live here?" I asked Mel.

She nodded. "On the other side of the stairs."

My eyebrows pinched together. While it's evident that Mel and Ace are related to each other, I don't think they are related to Caius, since all of Caius' features are dark, and all of Mel and Ace's features are light. They were opposites in every sense. I found myself wondering why she lived *here,* instead of… not here.

"Should we get started?" Mel exhaled, bringing me out of my thoughts as she moved to her bag that was placed behind the bathroom door. She pulled out a curling iron, hair clips, and a few other hair products. I could hear the clatter of makeup pallets falling against each other in her bag as she continued to dig around.

I stood with my hands at my side, unsure what to do with myself. "I'm going to be honest with you here, Mel. I have no idea what tonight is."

A giant smile spread on her lips as she unraveled the cord to the curling iron and plugged it into the wall by the mirror.

She turned to face me, her hands leaning on the edge of the countertop behind her.

"It's the annual Open House."

"Open House?" I furrowed my eyebrows. "What is that?"

Mel shook her head. "I'm not supposed to tell you anything else. Cai's orders."

Caius. The fact that she calls him Cai tells me they are close, and he must trust her if he let us both use his bathroom. And the underlying meaning of him putting me in *this* bathroom instead of Mel's did not slip away from me.

"Are you going, too?" I asked, even though she already looked ready to go. Her blonde hair fell in soft waves to the middle of her sides, and her makeup was already completely done. Even though she was in grey sweatpants and a zip-up hoodie, she could still walk into the party right now and look better than most people there.

She shrugged and looked over her shoulder to the curling iron, checking the heat. "I'll probably make an appearance. But I've been to it so many times, it's boring to me now."

She looked back to me as she picked up the curling iron, snapping its clamp. "But you, Miss Castell," she stepped behind me and placed her head over my shoulder, looking at my reflection in the mirror. "You will not be bored tonight."

Caius

"You know, my wife and I were thinking of sharing a mausoleum. Maybe a side-by-side sort of thing."

I swirled the drink in my glass before taking another sip. The ice was melting, and the liquid was growing warm. I winced at the watered-down piss flavor.

"Would that be possible?"

I nodded my head and flashed a quick grin. "Of course it's possible, Mr. Hawke."

The party had only begun thirty minutes ago, and I was already answering the same damn questions over and over. It was like a playback track in my head, and all I had to do was push one of the preprogrammed buttons of answers. It was mindless conversation at this point.

But these were potential clients, and I had to keep my business face on.

It's only one night out of the year, after all.

I pretended to play with one of the cuff links on my suit jacket as Marcus Hawke proceeded to talk to me about his interest in this place and his desire to spend his eternity here.

If you were to ask anyone about their thoughts on the afterlife, most people have the same outlook.

Heaven, Hell, sometimes Purgatory.

If you're good, you go to Heaven. If you're bad, you go to Hell. If you believe in Jesus Christ, you go to Heaven. If you don't, you go to Hell.

Pretty cut and dry, right?

But out of *all* those people, there's *always* that little nagging voice in the back of their head that gives them doubt. They don't have any definitive proof. They truly don't know where they will end up, no matter what they believe in. And if their beliefs aren't enough, then what happens?

Where do we go when we're not good enough?

It's a serious thought for everyone, and it's not to be taken lightly.

That's why my house is currently filled with people, *clients*, who want to control their outcome of the afterlife.

They want to hold the power in their hands.

And I'm here to give it to them.

Just as Mr. Hawke started to ramble on about the interior of his future mausoleum, a shimmer of white flashed out of the corner of my eye. I glanced over to see *her* walking through the groups of people.

Celeste Castell.

She was scanning the crowd, searching the faces in hopes of finding familiarity.

She was looking for *me*.

Her eyes finally caught mine, and I could see the breath hold in her chest. She was wearing the white silk dress I ordered for her, with her smooth, light brown skin exposed and her bare collarbones prominent. Her dark hair was curled in waves and cascaded down past her shoulders. Pieces were pinned back, giving me a full, open view of her face.

There was no umbrella, there was no hood, and there was no rain keeping me from seeing every inch of her delicate skin.

And with a half-smile to me from across the room, I knew this was the beginning of the end.

"Excuse me, Mr. Hawke," I gave a courteous nod as I turned to walk away, placing my old drink on a passing waiter's tray. Celeste didn't take her eyes off me as I made my way to her, ignoring everyone else who stood in my way.

When I approached her, she tilted her chin up to me, a brief grin flashing across her expression. Even with the heels, she was still shorter than me, causing me to look down at her soft, elegant features. I studied every piece of her, every pore, every beauty mark, every vitality in her eyes, and pressed it into the depths of my mind.

"You're here to give me that one last chance," I said with my voice lowered, letting the words rumble in the space between us.

She tilted her head playfully but kept her face neutral. "Make it count."

Fuck. If she didn't already know she had me wrapped around her finger, she'll find out tonight.

From across the room, I heard a few clinks of glass. Ace had grabbed a chair and stood on its seat, with a butter knife in one hand and glass of champagne in the other. Chatter from the party dissolved, and I could hear Ace clear his throat.

"Welcome, everyone," Ace began. I kept my stare locked with Celeste's, unable to break the sudden trance she had me in.

"I want to thank you all for coming out tonight, and for taking an interest in us. In what we do here."

My eyes stayed on hers, and even though she continued to look at me, I could tell she was listening to what Ace was saying. Her eyebrows narrowed and she blinked, trying to focus on the subject matter.

"We take all of you seriously. We care about each and every one of you, and we honor and respect the life you give us."

Celeste's head snapped to the side, giving her complete attention to Ace's speech. My eyes lingered on her for a moment, probably a moment too long, before moving my thoughts over to Ace. A waiter came walking through the crowd, carrying a tray of champagne flutes. Quietly, I grabbed two and handed one to Celeste.

"I'd like to make a toast to the one who keeps this place running. The one who doesn't let anything slip through the cracks, the one who never makes a single mistake, the one who runs the tightest ship imaginable."

Ace scanned the room until his eyes found mine. With a superior grin, he raised his glass in my direction.

"To Caius Attila."

Celeste's eyes moved back to me. I could feel her stare, along with everyone else's, but her focus held something else.

Hesitation. Pause. Reluctance.

Fear.

The rest of the crowd raised their glasses along with him, cheering and wooing before downing their drinks. I nodded, forcing out a small smile before taking a sip of the champagne myself.

Celeste didn't drink.

"Now, if you will all make your way to the front corridor, the sun is almost set."

With the champagne flute still gripped in her hand, the bubbles streaming to the liquid's surface, Celeste stood completely still as the others filtered out of the room.

"You?" she asked, her voice shaken. Her eyes held a silent plea, a prayer, a beg for truth.

I said nothing as I watched her eyes glaze over with trepidation.

"You *run* Purgatory?"

My jaw tightened. Purgatory. She knew it was here, but she didn't know I was the one in charge. I made the decision to let her in on the secret, even though my brother didn't give me much of a choice, and her reaction wasn't unexpected. She fled from me, from the house, from the grounds, as anyone in their right mind would.

But she came back.

Even if it was just for her uncle, she came back. Her heart overpowered her mind, her grief conquered her beliefs, and her feelings defeated her senses. And if that happened once, it could happen again.

But with her new mistrust in me, I knew I only had a small amount of time to get through to her, and I could already feel the window closing. "Celeste," I started, and her chest heaved out an exhale. "It sounds a lot worse than it is."

She let out a huff, as if what I said was completely unbelievable. "I don't know, Caius," she pushed out, and my name on her tongue was like a spear to the lungs. "It sounds pretty bad."

She had no sympathy in her tone. Only frustration.

And that frustration was like fire in my veins.

"You're here, aren't you?" I asked, taking a step towards her, closing the small gap between us. "You're here to give me that final chance. So let me give it to you."

Celeste's light brown irises scanned mine, searching for an answer. Whatever she was looking for, she wasn't going to find it in me. She was going to find it in the land around her.

Her answers lie in the ghosts that roam, the fog that shields, the rain that waters.

Her answers lie in what she can see.

Everything else is just speculation.

"Come with me."

"But what about the party?"

"It's fine."

She tilted her head again. "What about everyone else?"

"*Fuck* everyone else."

She blinked at me, and I could tell she was hiding a sliver of a smile under her stone-faced expression.

"Ace can take care of it all. He knows exactly what to do."

I held my hand out to her, extending it as a peace offering, a guide, and an opening.

But mostly as a way to feel her skin on mine.

And when she placed her touch in the palm of my hand, everything in this world faded beyond all recognition. There was no brighter light than her. There was nothing that climbed higher than the lift she gave me. Everything in me—my blood, my bones, my soul—only existed in her realm.

I stood at the open door leading to the backyard. Caius had already stepped down onto the path, halfway into the darkness. Shadows covered the far side of his body, succumbing to the impending nightfall. My heartbeat raced as I lingered in the decision to go with him, or to stay.

"I promise, Celeste, nothing will happen to you."

I still wasn't sure why I was here. Why I was invited. Why I agreed to come.

Why, in every look he gave me, I felt safe.

Just as I was about to go with him, a voice spoke to my right. "You are the Celeste I've heard about."

I turned to see a middle-aged man, who was clearly a Catholic priest simply based on his attire, gold chasuble included. I gave him a polite smile and outstretched my hand in a shake. He took my palm in his but didn't move, holding it gingerly.

He heard about me? He knows who I am?

I tucked those thoughts away for another time.

"Nice to meet you," I replied, feeling Caius' stare on both of us. I knew he was annoyed at the interruption, but I really didn't mind. It was delaying whatever he had to show me.

"This is Father Nicholas," Caius bellowed out, introducing him in an act of intrusion. "He handles all of the services here."

My eyebrows raised at the job title as I dropped my hand. So, he was a Catholic priest who was *in on this?* He was okay with sending people to *Purgatory?*

Sounded like something that every Catholic priest would typically be against. My judgment got the better of me on this one.

"Will you keep him in line?" Father Nicholas asked, motioning to Caius, who slightly rolled his head back in irritation.

"I—"

Caius cut me off abruptly. "She is only here for the Open House as a guest, Father. She's not interested in committing."

My head tilted at his words. Sure, he was more than correct, but the fact that he jumped in so quickly to shut down the idea had my mind spinning.

Father Nicholas nodded at the realization, still looking at me. "Die with the Lord in your heart, and you will gain eternal life."

I gently smiled at the words I've heard thousands of times in Mass. I could practically recite the sentence in my sleep, and knowing how bored I used to get on Sunday mornings, I'm sure I did a few times.

Caius had clearly had enough of this conversation. "If you'll excuse us," he began, extending his hand palm up, waiting for me. He wanted to take me into the land of spirits, and I'd be crazy to not be at least a little bit terrified.

Before I could step down with Caius, Father Nicholas must have sensed my apprehension because he leaned over in my direction. "Here is a place that is unlike any other."

That was an understatement. But he said it with a deeply rooted grin, one that was so earnest, I couldn't push it away. I said my goodbyes to Father Nicholas as I took Caius' hand and stepped down onto the path. As an act of security, I inched as close as possible to Caius. I may be agreeing to whatever he wanted to show me, but I was still hyperaware of everything going on around us.

The edge of the sun's glow rested on the horizon, and I knew we only had minutes before the ghosts appeared. Anxiety rushed through the beat of my pulse, so I mentally tried to cling to Caius for support.

"So, how did you…" I began, my voice hushed, fear coating every syllable.

Caius must've noticed because his head turned to face me as we walked. A small smile formed on his lips. He was amused.

"How did you get this job?" I asked without looking at him. My eyes were scanning the area around us, waiting for the inevitable.

He chuckled. "This isn't a job."

This isn't a cemetery.

I squeezed my eyes shut, only briefly, as I tried to push away his words. Ever since the moment I met him, he has done nothing but try to tell me the truth. It was an odd realization.

Brushing a hand along his jaw, he continued. "I don't work here. I never have. This," he stretched out a hand, motioning to the grounds, "has been in my family for ages. It goes farther back than I could try to research."

We continued walking, and I listened.

"It was passed down throughout the years. My ancestors, my grandparents, my parents, and now myself. I grew up here."

I gave a confused look, quickly glancing his way. "Were you ever scared?"

He shook his head. "Never. The ghosts were always around. There was never a time when it didn't seem normal."

"Your parents didn't try to protect you from it?"

"Why would they? There was nothing to protect me from. There was no point hiding it from me if I only had to become desensitized to it later."

The concept was so foreign to me. A boy, now a man, that lived with ghosts every single night. He had answers to questions people fought their whole lives to discover.

And here he was, letting me in without hesitation.

Even though we were walking through the night, my heart surged with a new warmth.

Sliding his hands in his pockets, he continued. "Even when I learned that people were scared of ghosts and the afterlife, I didn't see it any differently. Death and what comes after just felt…natural."

"Technically, death *is* natural," I added. "But that doesn't mean things aren't mysterious or unexplainable."

"Unexplainable?" He looked to me as he cocked an eyebrow. "There is only one thing I can't explain to you, Celeste, and that's how my family came into this position in the first place. Everything else has an answer."

I took his words as a challenge as I followed his guided walk down the path. "Okay," I began, inhaling deeply. Just as I was about to speak, a light, shadowed figure found its way to the path. As it came closer, I saw that it was an elderly man who walked at a slow pace.

I held my breath, squeezing myself closer to Caius and away from the spirit.

I could sense Caius grinning as he pulled me closer, his arm snaking around my waist. It wasn't a romantic gesture, but a protective one.

And, I guess, that in itself was romantic.

The ghost continued on without paying us any mind.

"Can they see us?" I whispered.

"No."

"Can they hear us?"

"No."

"Do they know they're here?"

"Yes."

"Can they see at all? Can they see each other?"

"Considering the fact that they walk the paths, yes, they can see."

His arm left my waist, leaving the spot cold in its wake.

He continued. "But they never interact with each other. They don't even look at each other. So, no, they can't see one another."

I frowned. "Isn't that lonely?"

"Maybe," he said with a shrug. "But you're looking at it the wrong way. It's peaceful."

Peaceful. I thought about what it would be like to be here, to live here, to exist here in life after death. Everything was either a shade of grey or green, and everything was always wet.

But it was also quiet. And serene.

And relaxing.

But the thought of being alone for the rest of eternity felt worse than having peace.

"Can they do anything?"

Caius shook his head. "They can't. They can walk, and they can rest. That's it. They can't feel anything, touch anything, move anything. They only exist."

Caius took a left turn, and I followed, still with no idea where we were going. But at this point, we were far away from the house, with only the moonlight to illuminate the dampened path. I took in another breath as I spoke. "Why is it always raining here?"

"It's not," he said. "It's not raining right now, is it?"

My expression filled with annoyance, and he smiled.

"You mean, why is it always raining during the day?" he corrected. "Because that's how my family made Purgatory. There's no sun, there's no snow. There's no heat, there's no freezing temperatures. No summer, no winter, no seasons at all, actually. There's only the middle of it all. The between."

Between.

The word rang in my head like a bell. It made more sense than I cared to admit.

"Your family made it that way? Does that mean you have the ability to change it?"

He nodded slowly. "Technically, yes, but I have no desire to. Everyone who's here knows this is how it is, and they agreed to it. Consistency is what's fair. This is how it will be for the rest of time."

I looked down at the path, knowing he was right. As much as I'd like to think Uncle Russ could feel the sun on his skin, I knew he couldn't. This is what he chose.

"Why do they only come out at night?"

Caius sighed quietly through his nose, as if he was figuring a way to give me a simple answer. "It's one of the conditions."

I paused. "Conditions?"

Caius paused as well, his eyes meeting mine before turning to look ahead. I followed his gaze.

We reached the end of the path, and before us was a large, long building. Its walls, roof, and doors were all made of glass, making it completely see-through. Black steel beams made up the frame, just like Caius' house.

Even though it was nighttime, there was a soft glow coming from the inside. I squinted my eyes and leaned forward, trying to get a closer look.

"Come with me," Caius rumbled, placing his hand on the small of my back.

As soon as Caius opened the door and allowed me through, I was hit with a wave of warm humidity. It stuck to me like a second skin, and I immediately held my arms close to my chest.

But once I was completely in, I took a look around, only to have my breath taken away.

The inside was massive, with rows and rows of fresh greenery covering every inch of tabletop. Flowers lined the first few rows, with every color petal imaginable. There were white and purple lilies, pink and blue orchids, and bright red poinsettias. My eyes scanned all the colors, all the textures, and all the different shaped leaves. There was even an entire row dedicated to different colored roses.

"Oh my God," I began, my heart thumping, my eyes never moving away from all the different plants.

"This is the greenhouse," he stated proudly as he stood next to me, his eyes scanning all the plants. He had taken off his suit jacket and hung it up by the door, revealing a plain white button-down shirt. He rolled up the sleeves to his elbows, exposing strong, tattooed arms.

"This is incredible," I replied, still in awe of the intricacy and production of it all.

A set of misters on the ceiling clicked on, spraying the plants below it with a fine mist. The machines formed a line all the way down to the other side of the greenhouse, the setup ensuring every single plant below it got its water.

Caius stepped away and moved into one of the rows, his hands gently skimming against the damp, green leaves. I stood back at the door with my arms pulled up to my chest.

He turned to say something, but my absence surprised him. After finding me, he nodded his head and gestured for me to come with him, but I stayed where I was.

"I don't want to get wet."

He looked up to the sprinklers above and narrowed his eyes. "You won't. They're barely on."

Reluctantly, I walked into the row he was in. My hands dropped to my sides as I kept my attention on the flowers. They were so beautiful, so *vibrant,* I felt my heart warming and myself growing at ease in here.

With Caius at my side, I could feel his electricity surging in the space between us. He barely kept his distance, his arm almost touching mine, his large frame tall compared to my small one.

Reaching out, I touched a petal.

It was a purple petunia. Enchantment.

I moved to the next set of flowers, which were red geraniums. Happiness and love.

Down the row were blue orchids. Unique beauty.

I stopped at the flower. They were stunning, so perfect in their presentation.

But as I eyed them, I noticed the row of plants behind them.

They were white carnations. Just like the ones I brought here before.

Those are the flowers of God. And God isn't here.

With Caius at my back, I could feel his hand grab me tenderly, turning me to face him. The humidity was slick on my skin, causing a light layer of moisture to form on the surface.

But I was too focused on his stare to notice.

"It's for you."

I tilted my head. "What is?"

"This. The greenhouse."

His words were like an electric current through my body, pulsing my heart with adrenaline.

"I had it built the day after you came here for the first time. I saw you with the ivy, and the way your face lit up at the sight of it. So, I had it made and imported every kind of flower I could think of."

My breath stopped in the bottom of my lungs, swirling in astonishment.

"All of this, *Meum Caelum*. This is all yours."

His hand slowly brushed up my arm to my shoulder, his touch passing over the thin strap of my dress gently. He moved to my chin, his grasp delicate as he lifted my head up. A lock of dark hair fell over his forehead, his face covered in the fine mist as well. He closed the gap between us, our bodies pressed against one another.

My heart lurched into my throat as his grey eyes ached for me, with a need I've never felt, a bright need I've never seen in the darkness before.

I could feel that same ache hidden in the hollows of my being, trying its best to claw its way out.

With our eyes glued to one another, with the rush of blood beating throughout my body, I managed to speak. "How can this be real?"

Caius lifted a half grin. "Do you mean—"

I stopped him before he could finish. "Purgatory. This. How is this possible?" My voice hovered gently above a whisper, my tone mixing with the hiss of the misters. This was my vulnerability shining through in a sensitive moment.

"There are things in life that can never be explained, Celeste. The sooner you realize you'll never have all the answers, the sooner you'll have peace of mind about it. But in the unknown, there is familiarity. There is intimacy. There's perfection in mystery."

I could feel his free hand glide up the length of my arm. His touch skimmed my skin gracefully, creating invisible lines in the water that rested on the surface. Goosebumps broke through the humidity, piercing my pores in an act of defiance, as not one part of my body was cold.

There's perfection in mystery.

The heated look in his eyes was telling. There was a double meaning hidden in his words. He may have been talking about the afterlife, but I knew he was also referring to me.

As my heart continued to race, my hand moved up to his arm, resting gently in the crook of his bent elbow. I had a sudden desire to touch him, to move even closer to him, to squeeze myself into him more than I already was.

"You really did this for me?" I asked, my voice even quieter in my state of fascinated disbelief.

The hand that held my chin moved to my neck, with his thumb still on the side of my face. Reactively, I tipped my head back by a fraction.

Caius nodded, never tearing his eyes away from mine. "From the moment I saw you," he said, his tone deep and rich, "I knew I had to give you nothing less than everything."

And with that, he dipped his head low, closed his eyes, and pressed his lips to mine. Our souls as one, connected, entangled.

Every part of my body gave in to him and his ability to captivate me. My knees grew weak from the pressure of his lips, and a sultry fire began to kindle in the pit of my stomach. The feeling was breathtaking and enchanting. It was addictive.

He gently pulled away, leaving his lips to hover over mine as he slowly opened his eyes. When I managed to open mine, I found him watching me. His gaze was filled with adoration and reverence, a look I could never come to forget, no matter how hard I tried.

"Why do you do that?" he asked with his lips still brushing against the skin of mine, his tone somber yet quiet.

"Do what?" I responded.

The thumb that rested along the left side of my face gently stroked the damp skin. He pulled it away to reveal a swipe of makeup on the pad of his thumb.

"Hide yourself."

Instinctively, my own hand moved up, wiping away any moisture that lined the side of my face. I looked down at my fingertips only to see a layer of light brown concealer.

Panic set into my core at the realization. He was beginning to see me for who I really was and what parts of me I was trying to hide.

I opened my mouth to begin to explain myself, to explain the doubts that riddled my thoughts every day, but a knock sounded at the greenhouse door. Caius ignored it, with his stare still locked on me. He was waiting for my answer.

The door opened, and in walked the older man who was always stationed at the entrance. Lawrence.

"I'm so sorry to interrupt, Mr. Attila," he spoke sincerely. "Good evening, Miss Castell."

I gave a half smile, and he turned back to Caius.

"We have a slight inconvenience."

Caius

The air was cold against me, even though my insides were heated. I was fucking *furious*.

Weaving through the restless ghosts, I guided Celeste at my side in the path back to the house. Moments ago, her lips were on mine, sending me spiraling into the deepest version of need. I needed more of her, every part of her, all of her.

Every inch, every pore, every blood cell, every breath.

The second I saw her, I knew my life was no longer my own. She had me in a suffocating hold the instant her eyes met mine, even if she didn't know it.

And by some divine design, her body melded with mine in an act of connection.

But the fact that things were going well should've been a sign that everything was about to turn south.

With the quiet click of Celeste's heels next to me, I kept my hand on the small of her back, the silk of her dress soft under my palm as we walked briskly. I could tell she was having trouble keeping the pace, and I was moments away from lifting her and carrying her up to the house. But before I knew it, we were at the back door. I opened it and stepped through, keeping Celeste at my back in case of any surprises.

And boy, if I wasn't always *fucking* right.

In the main corridor, on an empty wooden chair, stood Amadeus, with an unopened bottle of champagne in one hand and a large kitchen knife in the other.

"There he is!" he shouted, waving the knife in the air at the sight of me. "And look, he brought *friends!*"

I watched as the insanity in his eyes bounced from me, to Lawrence, to Celeste, all in a matter of a second. I didn't think I could become more possessive and protective than I already was, but when I saw him look at her, I could feel the vigilance burning hot inside of me.

"Dey," I grumbled. "What are you doing here?"

Lawrence leaned over in my direction. "I tried to keep him out, Sir. He wouldn't take no for an answer."

"He's right," Amadeus chimed in. "I just had to see what all the fuss was about tonight. After all..." he began, clutching the handle of the knife. "It's been so long since I've been to one of these things."

"Because you're not invited," I pushed. "You haven't been allowed access to the Open House for almost ten fucking years now."

"Come on, bro. Lighten up. I'm only here to liven the party a bit. I want to tell everyone what they're *really* getting into."

I gently pushed Celeste behind me in an attempt to shield her from whatever shit Amadeus was trying to pull. I could feel her hands lightly grasp the back of my shirt, and the fact that she was in this position because of *me* pissed me off to no end.

In a swift motion, Amadeus swiped the blade of the knife to the neck of the champagne bottle, popping the cork off with a loud burst. I stood completely still as Celeste and Lawrence both flinched. The cork hit the ceiling with a thud, and foam spilled out of the bottle and onto the floor with a splat. Amadeus raised the drink, the bubbles pouring over his hand, and smiled.

"To Purgatory."

He took a swig of the drink, then threw the knife on the ground. I could hear Lawrence exhale.

"Lawrence," I requested, "take Miss Castell back to the group. Make sure she is safe and watched over."

Lawrence muttered a "Yes, Sir," the same time Celeste barked out a "Wait."

Amadeus looked over to her with a grin, and I turned my head to gaze at her over my shoulder.

"I want to hear what he has to say," she said, moving away from my back. Her voice was firm, and her shoulders were straight. She wanted answers, and she was going to get them from whoever was willing to talk. She wanted all sides to the story, not just mine.

"Celeste," I growled. "He is not the one you need to be listening to."

My eyes found hers in a plea attempt. She didn't know what she was about to get into, and I tried to convey that to her.

"What do you wanna know?" Amadeus interjected, taking another drink straight from the glass bottle.

"Amadeus, you need to leave. *Now.*" I raised my voice, but it didn't faze him. Instead, his face turned sour as he held his free hand up to me.

"Let the lady speak," he began, then stepped off the chair. "Don't you have any common courtesy?" He took a step toward Celeste, and in return, she took a step back. Amadeus took the hint and surrendered, remaining still in the spot he stood.

At least her guard is still up. I held back a grin. She can definitely hold her own.

"Who are you?" she asked.

"Amadeus Attila," he stated proudly. "Most people call me Dey. My family runs this shitshow. Or, should I say, *you* run it, right, brother?" He turned to me, his words laced with spite.

I could feel Celeste turn and look at me briefly before turning back to my brother.

My blood was fucking *boiling* at this point.

Her eyebrows narrowed as her expression turned confused. "You don't like it here?"

Amadeus let out a soft chuckle. "No. Never have."

"Why?"

He took another swig of champagne. "Because it's immoral."

"Dying and being laid to rest isn't immoral," she countered.

"No, but choosing to stay here is. Man doesn't deserve that much power. We deserve to be judged for our sins, and if we stay here, we escape judgment."

I fought every fucking urge to roll my head back and groan. This is why I didn't want him opening his mouth to her in the first place.

But, looking over, I could see the wheels in her head turning. She was taking his words and processing them, validating them, maybe even agreeing with them.

"Why aren't you allowed here?"

He shook his head. "I'm only banned from the annual Open House. I'm assuming it's because I actually stand against this place, and that's bad for business. Right, Cai?"

My expression remained blank as I forced my hand to stay at my side, rather than forming a fist to send in the depths of his face.

"Business?" Celeste echoed, turning to me. My gaze remained on my brother. If I looked at her now, I wouldn't be able to keep my emotions at bay. The softness that she brings out in me needed to stay dormant in this situation.

"Oh, he didn't tell you?" Amadeus cocked his head pompously. "You must be new here. Purgatory is a soul-sucking, life-fucking business that preys on the people it keeps."

God, I need to start fucking counting before I lose my shit. Ten... nine... eight...

"Do you know how much it costs to be buried here?" he asked Celeste, who turned back to face him and shook her head. *"Eight million dollars.* People are *paying* to give their souls to this place when they could be in Heaven instead."

"Or Hell," I chimed in.

"Even better," he lifted the champagne bottle. "Let the evil ones find a way out of their punishment."

"You need to go," I stated harshly, reaching my limit. "Now's not the time."

"Now's the *perfect* time," he added, stepping toward me, trying to get in my face.

"Caius," Celeste rasped out her interruption, and I immediately tore my attention away from my brother and onto her. Her eyes were glistening with an unknown fear, a deep trepidation, a growing hesitancy.

Because of *me.* Because of *this.*

"Is all of this true?" Her hands crossed over her arms, shielding herself.

I chose my words carefully. "True to him. Not to everyone else."

I watched as her eyes moved from Dey to me in an internal conflict that I couldn't hear. There were thoughts bubbling to the surface that she was refusing to bring to life.

Moving away from my brother and stepping to Celeste, I stood in front of her. Her skin still held its glow, and her eyes still continued to shine even through the constant contention deep in her chest.

"I see it in you," Amadeus started, speaking to Celeste from behind my shoulder. "I see your reluctance."

Her eyes moved off of me and to my brother. I kept my gaze on her, watching her as she toyed with the words he was feeding her.

"It's normal to feel the way you're feeling, because all of this isn't fucking natural. It's manipulation for the innocent, and it's concealment for the guilty."

It took every ounce of power in me, but I managed to shut out my brother's words. My eyes dropped to her throat as I watched her force down a nervous swallow. I lifted a finger to her arm, touching her hand in an act of sincerity. I didn't want her to think this night was all for nothing just because someone else got in her head.

She's a smart girl. She knows how to think for herself.

But in an environment like this, in a place full of unfamiliar unknowns, it was easy to get caught up in a false sense of security. One that isn't real to begin with.

Celeste turned to whisper to me. "I need to go," she hushed, her voice quiet enough to land on my ears only.

I nodded my head. Right now, the only thing I can do for her is to let her go.

But she'll be back. I know she will.

"Lawrence," I called, looking to him over my shoulder. "Escort Miss Castell to the valet and make sure she gets to her car without any issue."

He nodded. "Yes, Sir."

Her eyes found mine one final time as I dropped my hand from her arm. Taking a step toward me, she closed the space between us, leaned up, and planted her lips on my cheek. Her scent filled my lungs in an uncontrolled desire, a fragrance of bergamot and rose encasing me. I closed my eyes as I inhaled deeply, still aware of her embrace on me.

Her soul was still with me, despite her mind telling her otherwise.

And with that, she let me go. She turned away from me and followed Lawrence to the door. The white silk dress complimented her body beautifully, and my gaze remained locked on her effortless strides.

I turned back to Amadeus, who was mid-drink, his mouth suctioned to the opening of the champagne bottle.

"I don't want to see you at another Open House again."

He tipped the bottle to me, acknowledging my demand. "You got it, brother." He held a sense of satisfaction, along with pride in the fact that he got through to *someone.*

Then, in a second, I heard a shocked gasp from the other side of the room. My head snapped to see Celeste, looking through the doorframe, her hand covering her mouth.

"Uncle Lucas?"

I could hear the crack in my voice as I stared at the tall, brown-haired man in front of me. The party was still in the long, windowed corridor, but now everyone was back to mingling and drinking. Uncle Lucas dressed nicer than I've ever seen him before, even better than the outfit he wore to his own brother's funeral, as he wore a dark grey suit that was tailored to fit him perfectly. He was talking to another woman, and whether she was someone he came here with or not, I didn't care, nor did I want to find out.

"Uncle Lucas?" I repeated, as if he was an illusion I could make disappear by the sound of his name.

He turned to me, the blood draining from his face, his skin turning a shade of pale. "Celeste?" he spoke with the same tone of disbelief as me. "What are you doing here?"

I wanted to ask him the same thing, but I didn't have to.

Because I knew.

He wanted to be buried here, just like Uncle Russ.

That was the whole purpose of the Open House, right? To come here, to watch the ghosts, to figure out if this is a good fit for your soul in the afterlife?

Do you want to spend the rest of eternity's days in this plot of land? Do you want to watch the rain, feel the mist, endure the fog for all of infinity? Do you want to wander the paths at night with no purpose, no life, no feeling? Do you want to stay here until time doesn't exist? Until we all reach the end of the world, the end of this realm and the realm that is built here?

Do you want to be alone?

"You shouldn't be here," Uncle Lucas took a step toward me, reaching for me, but I pulled away.

"Neither should you."

The woman that Uncle Lucas was with had walked away, moving on to someone else to talk to. I could feel a warm presence at my back, and without looking, I knew it was Caius. I could sense his ambient energy, even without him saying a word, but I chose to ignore him for the time being.

"Celeste," Uncle Lucas echoed, but his request to defend himself fell on my deaf ears.

"Did you always know?" I asked.

"Know what?"

"About this. About what happens here. About Uncle Russ choosing this."

He wondered for a moment, then shook his head. "No, not always."

I gave him a look that implied I needed an explanation.

"He told me about it about a month before he died, right before his decline. I didn't believe him at first, but when I came here for the burial, I knew he was telling the truth. I could feel it."

I sighed quietly. I knew the exact feeling he was talking about because I could feel it, too.

The essence of the living earth mixed with the elements of the afterlife.

The unknowns colliding with familiarity.

The comfort of the inevitable grief.

But even though the pull was there, that didn't mean he needed to consider being buried here, too.

Without asking him to, I knew he was going to try and justify his reasoning for being here tonight, and I didn't want to hear it. I didn't want to know why he was taking an interest in this place.

Then again, I was here tonight, too. I may not wonder about my afterlife just yet, but I still had a nagging fascination that brought me back here, time after time.

It was the constant state of mental tug-of-war. Sometimes, this place gave freedom; sometimes, it gave restrictions. Sometimes, it gave power; sometimes, it took it away.

Sometimes, it was soothing; sometimes, it was terrifying.

"Why did he choose this?" I asked.

A softness reached Uncle Lucas' face, one that I've never seen before. It was a type of sadness that he had never expressed, at least not around me.

"I don't know. I wish I did."

In his words, the sounds laced with sympathy and regret, I knew he was being honest. And that's the part that hurt him the most.

His expression returned back to normal as he glanced to Caius, and then back to me. His eyes scanned over my dress briefly, and I watched as he squeezed his eyes shut in annoyance. "You really shouldn't be here, Celeste."

"I'm fine," I bit out. If there's one thing I hate most, it's being babied. I can take care of myself, and I don't need anyone else making or judging my decisions.

"Your dad would kill me if he knew."

I paused. "Does he know about all this, too?"

Uncle Lucas looked down to the ground, and his hand moved up to the back of his neck, rubbing the skin gently. There was an awkward silence between us, and I let it settle before asking again.

"Uncle Lucas, does he know?"

He shook his head. "No. Russ only told me."

Oh, shit. Now I'm caught in the middle of a family secret that only Uncle Lucas and I know, and the weight of my parents not knowing is now on my shoulders. And if Uncle Lucas *does* decide to be buried here when the time comes, my dad is probably going to want to be here, too. If not, he's definitely going to at least look into it. And if he looks into it, he'll figure the rest out.

"Let me take you home," Uncle Lucas suggested, reaching for me once more, but I avoided him again.

"No. My car is here. I can drive myself."

His eyes glanced back to Caius once again, who still hadn't moved from the spot behind me.

I cleared my throat in an attempt to get his attention back on me. "I'll go if you go."

Uncle Lucas hesitated for a moment as he weighed his options, but then nodded. "Yeah, alright."

I accepted my fate and acknowledged the fact that this was the end of my night. Before stepping away to leave, I managed to turn and look over my shoulder slightly. Caius was there, his hands in his pockets, watching me. Thank God I already gave him a kiss goodbye, because there was no way I was about to do it now in front of my uncle.

But in that moment, he leaned down to my ear, his lips only a fraction of an inch away from my skin.

"This isn't over, Celeste."

His voice ripped through my insides, heating every morsel of my being in a fire for him.

He knew I would be back.

He knew this night was only the beginning.

Hollowed choruses rang through the massive, ancient cathedral as the congregation sang the hymns. The echoed voices bounced off the walls, creating a reverb in the sanctuary. It was a beautiful sound, but my mind refused to focus.

How can we all sing, pray, and listen to topics about the afterlife when some of us don't plan on being there? Why even bother?

There are people that sing about God and Heaven, yet don't believe it's the path for them. They would rather sign themselves away to Purgatory for the rest of time.

Although, I have no idea if anyone from the party is here now. I didn't get a look at anyone's face besides Uncle Lucas, and he never goes to mass.

But my Uncle Russ always went to mass with us every Sunday. Apparently, it didn't matter to him.

To my left, my parents stood together, holding and sharing a hymnal as they sang together. To my right, Serena cradled Nolan, swaying and bouncing him in an attempt to get him to calm down. He was fussy, and I would be, too, if I had to sit through Catholic Mass with my teeth cutting through my gums. I reached over and grabbed his hand, my pointer finger fitting perfectly in his little palm, and he instinctively held on. I gave him a big, cheesy smile, and it seemed to help for a bit.

That is, until the organ stopped playing, and the room went quiet.

Nolan began to fuss again, and Serena looked to me, her dark hair up in a bun and her brown eyes tired.

"I'm going to step out. I'm not sure if I'll be back."

She was still acting bitter toward me, and since I never gave her a real apology for snapping at her the other day, her cold shoulder was to be expected.

I nodded in understanding, but then quickly reached for her arm. She stopped and turned to look at me.

"I need to talk to you at some point."

She narrowed her eyes at me, confused. "Is everything okay?"

"Yeah," I assured. "Just call me sometime this week."

She nodded, and I watched as she exited the pew. She silently made her way down the rows, and as I looked over my shoulder, my gaze fell on someone standing three pews back. He was wearing a black button-down shirt and black dress pants, with his hands clasped together in front of him.

Caius.

His dark hair fell perfectly over his forehead as he made eye contact with me, like he was waiting for me to notice him. I immediately turned back around with my heart lurching up into my throat and my pulse speeding.

What was he doing here? Was he *allowed* here? Does he believe in any of this?

I swallowed my sudden nerves down and placed my hands on the frame of the pew in front of me. I gripped the polished wood, trying to balance myself and my mind.

My mom leaned over and whispered, "Are you okay?"

I made sure to keep my body still and straight, keeping Caius from reading any sort of body language. "Yeah, I'm fine," I answered.

The priest called for us to sit, so we did. I tucked my dress under my legs and smoothed it out over my thighs, fiddling with the fabric nervously in hopes that Caius wasn't watching me.

But I knew he was. I could feel his stare against my shoulders, on the back of my neck, and down my spine.

I could feel it through the rest of the service. Through the head-bowed prayers, through the mindless reciting, and through the communion that I couldn't bring myself to partake in.

Every time I closed my eyes, I was brought right back to last night, and I could practically feel his lips in his kiss. I could feel his lingering touch on the back of my neck, his thumb on my cheek, his chest pressed up against mine. It felt like an eternity ago as I crossed my legs uncomfortably, trying to squash any wistful memory of him while sitting in a *church*.

"Delight each anointment to Heaven." The priest spoke, and the congregation echoed an "Amen" into the air. With that, mass was over. My parents shuffled out of the pew and turned to me.

"I'm going to check on Serena," my mom said softly. "Do you want to go get lunch?"

I shook my head. "Thanks, but I have too much to do back at home. Maybe next week?"

My mom nodded, and my dad slipped back into the pew to say goodbye. He leaned down and planted a kiss on the top of my head while I remained sitting.

"Love you, baby girl."

"Love you, too," I responded to both of them, then watched as they turned to go. They walked down the center aisle and out of sight.

With a sigh, I looked down at my hands in my lap. The hem of my black dress was beginning to fray, and I started to pick at the seams as my mind started to wander. For some reason, I couldn't stick to one single thought, but there was a common denominator in them all.

Caius.

As if he could read my mind, he slipped into the pew behind me, his presence unignorable. He remained silent as he sat down, the smell of his woodsy musk entering my lungs with each inhale. I kept my head down, the waves of my hair falling along the sides of my face in a curtain.

I could feel Caius lean forward, his knees hitting the prayer cushion along the bottom of the frame behind me. He was acting as if he was deep in prayer, but his demeanor said otherwise.

"Celeste," he rasped, darkness coating the aura around us, sinking me down into his depths.

My name on his tongue created a slight hum in my body. His lips were so close to my ear, that I could feel his breath on my skin, creating instant goosebumps on every inch of me.

Reaching up, he gently brushed away the hair from my face, pushing it back over my shoulder. I could see him out of my peripherals as I kept my head and eyes down. My chest began to heave as I struggled to catch my breath.

I found myself aching for him, for his touch, for his desires.

His hand reached around and found the front of my throat. His palm rested there for a moment, feeling the bare skin and the light pulse of my heart before moving up to my chin. He gently pushed my head up, forcing me to tilt back and into his territory. I scanned the rest of the pews and quickly noticed that no one was paying us any mind. There were a few people scattered throughout the sanctuary, but all were faced forward with their heads bowed. The priest entered the confessional, attending to someone on the other side.

Caius squeezed the bottom of my jaw, bringing my attention back to him. My eyes fell closed, succumbing to the fire in his touch.

His face rested along the side of my neck, his lungs breathing me in, his need for me unrelenting.

"You didn't take your communion, *Meum Caelum,*" he whispered against my skin. I didn't have time to think about what his foreign words meant before he directed my gaze to the communion in front of me. There was a small white cracker and a small cup of red wine. It remained on top of the Bible that was tucked away in the pew in front of me.

"Is there a reason why you don't want it?"

After a moment passed, I tried to shake my head but struggled in his hold.

"Are you scared?"

I shook my head again.

"Do you believe in it?"

My body remained still. *Do I?* My whole life, I've taken communion without a second thought. Sometimes, I did it mindlessly, and sometimes, I acknowledged the weight of it. But no matter what, I've always taken it as truth.

What made today so different?

Leaning over my shoulder, Caius reached for the small, circular cracker. With his other hand, he squeezed the hollows of my cheeks, forcing my lips to part and my mouth to open slightly.

"Give me your tongue," he began, his voice soft in volume but firm in tone.

I obeyed and dropped my tongue out of my mouth. Caius placed the wafer on the flat of my tongue, his grip still tight on my jaw, his skin brushing against mine in a heated desire.

"Corpus," he muttered, his deep voice rumbling to my core. "The Body."

Bringing my tongue back into my mouth, I let the soft wafer dissolve and swallowed it down.

"Good girl," he whispered, and I instantly squeezed my eyes shut at his praise, my own yearning growing stronger by the second.

Next, he reached down and grabbed the small cup of wine. My eyes opened to see him lifting the clear plastic to his own gaze, his focus on the liquid as he swirled it around.

"Sanguis," he said, and I could hear the slip of a smile through his tone. "The Blood."

He was enjoying this.

But so was I.

He brought the cup to my lips, the lips that were still clutched in the tight grasp of his hand. I moved to take only a sip, but as he angled the cup up higher, I had no choice but to down it all. Drips of red wine spilled out from both corners of my mouth, streaming down my chin, neck, and over the tips of his fingers.

He dropped the empty cup, and the plastic clattered on the wooden pew. Thankfully, no one heard the sound, but if they did, everyone remained facing forward.

Caius removed his hand from my face, releasing his grip on my jaw. Moving his mouth to my chin, he kissed my skin, licking and sucking the excess wine that drew crimson-colored lines down my neck. The feel of him in an area so sensitive, so exposed, so vulnerable had me in the deepest vault of passion. I angled my throat to him more, allowing more access to his intimacy, letting him take me for all I was. With his hand still cradling the other side of my neck, his lips and tongue both caressed the wine off my skin, leaving no area untouched.

My breathing was rapid but steady as his actions took my body to higher places. I could feel my insides burning with a flame that only he could blaze.

My hands reached up and found his as he continued to drink me in, and my body shifted at the new, increasing fervor. Part of me wanted all of him, right *here*, right *now*, but the other part of me knew this wasn't the time or place.

Obviously.

His mouth trailed down to my collarbones in a line of licks and kisses. My fingers ran through his hair, gently gripping and pulling, eager to move him closer to me.

A hint of a moan escaped my lips between breaths. *"Caius."*

Then suddenly, as quickly as this all started, he stopped. His lips and breath hovered over my skin for a moment before he pulled away, leaving my exposed skin cold in his absence.

He leaned up to my ear, and my eyes closed at the sensation.

"See you soon," he whispered, then stood to leave.

Too shocked to fully turn around, I slowly glanced over my shoulder. I watched as he adjusted his rock-hard cock and brushed off any debris from the knees of his pants.

Then, without another word, he exited the pew and walked out the church doors, leaving me in my dying flame.

Celeste

Thursday. Three o'clock.

I stepped up into my uncle's mausoleum. It's been over a month since his burial, and the inside looks as if everything was put together just yesterday.

No dust, no dirt, no leaves, no rainwater on the floor.

Only perfection in the form of a soul-encasing building.

The dim shine of the stained-glass windows illuminated my body, barely reflecting in the gloomy daylight as I made my way to the counter. My fingers hardly skimmed the surface before the sound of the rainfall suddenly muted, and I knew there was something, someone, blocking the entryway.

There was absolutely no denying that my pulse had been racing from the moment I stepped out of my car, simply at the possibility that he'd be here.

At the possibility that he'd come out to see me.

At the possibility that his lips would find my skin again.

And just the sound of the disappearing raindrops had my stomach sinking, my heart skipping, my lungs tightening.

I turned around to see him already inside the mausoleum, with his hood pulled down and his eyes glinting with need.

He took a single step toward me, and I could feel a heavy breath catch in my throat.

"Caius," I squeezed out, my voice quiet and aching.

That was the only word I managed to get out before he closed the gap between us. He wasted no time in rushing to me, grabbing me behind my thighs, and picking me up. My legs circled his waist, my arms wrapped around his neck, and his lips found mine. There was an authentic passion radiating from him, one that could not be contained. I could feel him pour out his entire soul into our kiss, with his tongue meeting mine and his chest firmly planted against my body.

He led me to one of the stone benches along the side wall. Placing me down on the cement gently, he was careful not to hurt me as he lowered himself. My arms remained around his neck as he kneeled down in front of me.

"When you say my name," he began, seriousness etched in his voice, "I lose every bit of self-control I've come to know."

He unzipped his jacket and threw it to the floor. Rain droplets scattered throughout the inside of the mausoleum as I looked down at his plain grey t-shirt. I paused, a confusion hitting me briefly. Have I ever seen him wear a plain shirt before?

That thought didn't matter, because in a second's time, he ripped that shirt off and threw it, revealing smooth, inked skin and tight, firm muscles. Glancing down, I noticed the realistic portrait of the Angel of Grief tattooed across the span of his chest, along with other intricate patterns highlighting the rest of him. I ran my hands over his skin, feeling the seamless ink under my fingertips. His eyes glimpsed down to my touch, reveling in the image of our skin together.

Reaching up, he took off my jacket and tossed it with his. Underneath, I was still wearing my white work shirt from the coffee shop, but he didn't seem to care. His lips found mine again as his hands slid up and down my arms, his touch needing fulfillment in my skin. I moved to sit higher, never letting our lips disconnect as my palms found the sides of his neck, the heat of his pulse flowing under my grasp.

"Caius," I pressed against his lips, letting only the sound of his name escape between breaths. His hand found the back of my head and gripped my loose, wavy hair, tugging my head back forcefully.

"I told you," he said, his face only an inch from mine, *"my name on your lips reduces the rest of this world to nothing, Celeste."*

I could feel a slight shiver run through my body at the sound of my own name. Our words have the same effect on each other, it seemed.

He tugged my hair again, this time with more pull. I looked up at him through my narrowed eyelids, waiting for him to give in to what we both needed.

His eyes met mine, his grey irises cold and daunting as the sound of the rain continued on. "In all my life, I've always held my composure. Always."

His fingers loosened, but only for a second before tightening again. I could feel the muscles in his shoulders constrict beneath my wrists.

"Until *you.*"

He didn't say it with fault. He didn't blame me.

He said it with a want so urgent, a desire so deep, I could feel its purity in my veins.

"The moment you said my name in that church, *Meum Caelum,* I almost threw you down and fucked you right there."

I shuddered at the image, the space between my thighs growing wet.

"In the pew, with others around, right under the eyes of Mother Mary."

With my head still pulled back and his face close to mine, my lips parted at his words.

"And now, the very first thing you say to me is my name, as if you're *begging* for me to rip you open from the inside out."

His free hand moved to my knee, then to the inside of my thigh, then up between my legs. I knew he could feel the heat through my jeans, because the look in his eyes grew even more intense than moments before.

"Is that what you want?" he asked, and all I could do was stare at him. "Is that why you say my name with a velvet tongue?"

My breath danced on his lips as I inched closer, letting my skin lightly brush on his. He remained still, waiting for my answer in words, but all I could give him was an answer in my actions.

My nose skimmed against his as I taunted him with a kiss, my eyes flickering down to his lips before closing completely. I could feel his anticipation in his posture, his expectations in his demeanor.

I was the one in control. He was the one losing it.

And as my hands roamed all over his body, from his neck to his shoulders to the bottom of his bare back, I said one word.

"Caius."

With that, he grabbed the bottom of my work shirt, ripped it off, and threw it to the floor, leaving me in my black bra. His hands moved to my jeans, and with a quick pull, popped the button off. The damp air hit my skin, creating a small array of goosebumps along my torso as he pulled the denim off my legs.

There I was, on the concrete bench of my uncle's mausoleum, in only my bra and underwear. There wasn't a single ounce of hesitation in me, even with the black vase sitting in the corner of my vision.

Caius dipped his head down to my neck, his lips finding and sucking the sensitive skin. I angled my head away from him, giving him better access to me. His hands quickly grabbed his belt, and with a swift motion, he pulled it right off.

My breath was heavy, and my need was heavier. I could feel the humidity on our skin, mixing with one another, already creating a closeness that could only be heightened.

His hands gripped the top of my underwear, causing my skin to tense under his touch. He tore those off, too, and threw them without looking up from my neck. My hands fumbled with his jeans, and with a bit of his help, we both managed to get everything down in a few seconds.

And without warning, without a second of indecision, he lined himself up at my entrance and slid his throbbing length inside of me. I let out an aroused yelp, but quickly covered my mouth when I realized we were still somewhat out in the open.

Caius released his mouth from my skin, only to move it up to my ear. "Don't worry. It's only us."

His hips slammed into me again, and I couldn't help but let out another cry.

It was a song of pleasure, a melody of passion.

With each slick thrust, I could feel myself descending into his realm, collapsing into the world of Caius Attila.

The place I *wanted* to be.

"*Holy fuck,*" he growled, the sound only increasing my lust. He leaned back, tilting his body away from me, and tried to get a deeper angle. The colored lights from the stained glass window illuminated his tattooed body, adding different hues to the pictures under his skin. He lifted his head back in pure ecstasy, and pieces of his hair fell off his damp forehead.

It was an otherworldly vision, and it was a divine feeling.

He continued to pump into me, and I could feel his lengthened cock fill me completely. Our hips found a steady rhythm, one that played my body so effortlessly.

Leaning down, he moved to kiss me once more, ending the embrace with my bottom lip between his teeth. Then, after letting it go, he pressed his forehead to mine.

"There is nothing, nor will there ever be anything that compares to you, Celeste." His dark, hushed words hit me in a spot so deep, so defenseless, that I had no choice but to embrace it.

His cock throbbed inside of me, and I knew he was close to finishing. My legs wrapped around his smooth waist again, as the sweat and humidity mixed together on our skin to create the perfect slick combination.

I used my hands to prop myself up on the bench as he moved to pull me close to him. The angle created a new friction between us, one that hit the direct spot I needed to send me into an extreme ecstasy. It felt as if a rip tide soared through my body, pulling me in waves, pushing me to the curve of the crest. And judging by the sudden shudder in his body, I knew Caius was riding that wave with me.

Our bodies as one, our souls intertwined.

We were here in this realm, together, in the space between the pleasures of Heaven and the tortures of Hell.

I came down from the high of our orgasm with a loss of breath and an increase of emotion. I felt pleased, confused, satisfied, and dazed.

Everything happened so fast, so quick, I didn't have a chance to think about anything twice.

I didn't have a chance to let my mind catch up with my body.

I didn't have a chance to let my thoughts override my needs.

I'm glad I never had that chance, because as Caius finally looked back up at me, a slight smirk formed on his lips.

I would do it all again. And again. And again.

I needed him in the valleys of my soul and in the peaks of my spirit.

I needed him, and there was no going back.

Caius

"Can I ask you something?" she said as she walked along a row of flowers, her fingers skimming along a petal.

"Anything," I replied, trailing close behind her.

We found ourselves in the greenhouse, making our way through the endless rows of greenery. I offered to take her up to the house after fucking her completely raw, but she wanted to come here first. I happily obeyed her requests, but only after I gave her my grey shirt to wear. Now, I walked with her in just my jeans and rain jacket, which I only zipped up halfway.

"Your brother," she began, a bit hesitant. "What happened?"

I narrowed my eyes. "You'll have to be a bit more specific, Celeste."

She took a deep breath, pausing at a white and red carnation. "Why doesn't he believe in this like you do? He grew up with you here, right?"

I nodded. "He did, but he never liked it. Ever. He didn't like the spirits, and he didn't like the death that accompanied them. Ever since he was old enough to understand what went on here, he never wanted to be part of it."

"So, he just… wasn't?"

I shook my head. "He moved out as soon as he was eighteen. He joined a church, and that's where he felt like he belonged."

As she looked back down to the flower, I could see the wheels in her head turning again. Her soft, dark hair fell over her face, and her hand moved up to tuck it behind her ear. Her cheeks were flushed, her eyes were delicate, and the tip of her nose was red.

Fuck, she was so *fucking* beautiful.

"Church?" she asked, her eyebrows slanting downward.

"Yeah," I started. "He was always opposed to Purgatory, but after he joined his church, that's when he *really* began to speak out against it. And every time I see him, his hatred for all this grows. He'll show up at the most inconvenient times to let me know that his opinion hasn't changed, as you saw."

She chuckled softly, but the sound quickly faded. "Yeah, I remember." Her voice trailed off, and I could tell she was growing timid in her questions. "Have you ever started to agree with him?"

"Never."

"Why not?"

I sighed. "Because, Celeste, I believe in free will. I believe in choices. I believe in holding the power of our next life while still living in this one."

"You don't think God should be the one to choose for us?"

"I think God gives us the intelligence to choose for ourselves."

Her eyes moved to find mine, and I caught her stare. She showed a hint of hopefulness, a sliver of belief, and I locked into it.

There was no part of me that wanted to *convince* her that any of this was the absolute correct way. I'm not interested in that. Because along with my belief in choice, I believe in the freedom to choose the other outcome.

But in that sense, I'm going to do my best to open her eyes to what I know she already believes in.

I can see it in her. She thinks the same as me.

She sees that freedom. She sees the opportunity in taking the power and honing it into the next life.

She wouldn't be here, with me, if she didn't.

With a quick but subtle shake of her head, she turned back around and grabbed the stem of a carnation, pulled it out from the soil, and cradled it in her palm.

"And your parents?" she asked, dusting the excess dirt off the flower.

"They both died about five years ago in a car accident."

Celeste quickly turned to me, a look of worry in her expression, as if she was sorry for bringing it up. I quickly brushed it off because there was nothing for her to feel sorry for. Time heals.

"They left Purgatory to me in their will. Originally, it was to go to both Dey and me, but after he clearly wanted nothing to do with it, they changed their will. They knew he would sell it."

We began walking back to the door, and she tilted her head to me. "Sell it?" she asked curiously. "You can do that?"

"If I wanted to, yes."

"Are there a lot of people that want to buy it?"

I shook my head as I walked with her, side by side, my hands in my pockets. "I've gotten offers a few times. And my parents were right; Dey would've taken the first one. No doubt about it."

"You don't ever consider it?"

"No. Never."

And that was that. Celeste accepted my answer for what it was without any rebuttal. My words were final, and she knew it.

As she reached for her jacket, I placed my hand on her arm, stopping her. "Wait," I eased, causing her to pause. "There's something I want to show you."

Celeste looked at me, intrigued.

"I didn't have a chance to show you during the Open House before we were… interrupted." I motioned to the carnation in her hand. "Leave that here."

Celeste obeyed and gently balanced the flower on the door handle. Following my lead, I guided her to the end of one of the rows of flowers. Against the back wall was a frosted glass door, one that blended in with the rest of the steamed, misted glass if you didn't know it was there. Resting my hand on the black metal handle, I moved to the side and let Celeste step in front of me. She glanced at me, confused, as I opened the door and let her through.

Inside was a large, open, circular room. The walls and domed ceiling were made of clear glass, just like the central area of the greenhouse. Plants lined the metal frame, with ivy twisting up the metal, sprawled leaves decorating the floor, and buds of different flowers beginning to bloom in the fine mist. The greenery was heavy throughout the room, creating a natural, comforting nest.

But the real vision lies in the center of the room. Right there, in the middle of the floor, was a pond-like pool with a curved, stone edge and white tile along the sides. A small slope formed in the opening, allowing the ability to gradually walk into the water. As a small handful of lily pads floated on the surface, the greenery reflected off the water, casting the clear liquid in a beautiful teal glow.

Celeste's breath was heavy next to me as I stared at her, watching her react to my gift to her. I wasn't lying when I told her that everything, all of this, was only for her. There wasn't a doubt in my mind when I decided to have this built the day after I saw her. I wanted her to have a space that she could call her own, one that she could come to whenever she wanted. One that kept her away from the noise of Purgatory.

Watching her face light up at the sight of this made everything worth it.

And feeling her hand grab mine sealed the fate of my soul in her.

With our fingers intertwined and my eyes still on her, I brought her hand up to my lips, kissing her knuckles. She finally looked over to me, the glow in her happiness still radiant.

"For me?" she whispered.

"For you," I answered, my lips still pressed to her hand.

Letting me go, Celeste approached the side of the pool. She kneeled down, letting her knees rest along the edge of the stone, and reached her hand to the water. The tips of her fingers barely broke the surface as she waved through the water, ripples forming in their wake. I watched as my grey shirt hung loosely off her shoulders, blanketing her silhouette, and I could feel the heat rise in myself once again.

The way her hair fell so gently along the side of her face, the way her head tilted at her own reflection in the water, the way the corner of her mouth lifted in a grin.

I'm in so fucking deep.

"No one has access to this room except for you."

She looked back. "Only me?"

I nodded.

"Not Ace? Or Mel?"

"No."

"Not the ghosts?"

"The ghosts are only allowed on the paths and in their own mausoleums. Nowhere else."

She paused, digesting my words and filling in the empty spaces between them. "That's one of the… conditions?"

I nodded again.

"What about you?" she asked, rising to her feet and stepping toward me. "Do you have access to this room?"

I cleared my throat as she neared me, trying to keep my shit together. "Only if you want me to."

Once she finally reached me, her hand slid up to the side of my neck, her touch warm against me. She stood on her tiptoes, eager to meet me as she brushed her lips against mine. Without kissing me, she dangled the lust in front of me, toying with me.

It took all of my might, all of my self-control, to not grab her and crash into her.

"Caius Attila," she began, the pronunciation of my name forcing her tongue to slip past her own lips and lightly touch mine. *Holy fuck,* if I didn't lose it right then and there at the sound of my full name. "You have twenty-four-seven access to this room."

That did it for me. I grabbed the back of her neck, kissed her, and took her.

Caius

Celeste put on her jacket as we reached the door, then picked up the carnation from the door handle. After I zipped my own jacket, we both pulled up our hoods and walked outside.

The rain was at a steady downfall, as always, but in this moment, it was refreshing. My skin was still heated and slick with sweat, my muscles were tired from our compromising positions, but my dick was more than ready for round three. And if she tries to say my name with the strike of her tongue again, I won't hesitate to make it happen.

There was something about the way it fell off her lips, the way the syllables were coated with a silk-sounding tone, the way her voice smoothed the inside walls of my chest.

There was no way to explain it, and I had no desire to try to find the words for it.

We made it a few steps before Celeste stopped. I paused with her, confusion striking my face.

"What?" I asked, my gaze landing on the leftover blood rush to her cheeks.

"Are they here?"

"Who?"

"Your parents."

I slowly inhaled, my mind now directing my thoughts in a different direction. "Yes."

"Do they…"

I didn't hesitate to finish her question. "Walk around at night? Yes."

"Is it weird?"

I shrugged. "It was at first. But now, it's normal."

She nodded slowly, and I could tell she was contemplating something. I waited, expecting her to say something as the rain fell between us.

Her voice was quiet, only slightly above a whisper as she spoke. "Can you take me to them?"

I froze. It was such a simple request, a harmless one at that. But no one had ever cared enough to see them, to know anything about them, or to take any sort of interest in them.

In fact, no one really takes an interest in Purgatory at all unless it's for their own benefit.

I looked at her, our eyes matching a buried apprehension that couldn't be explained. She was diving deep into this world, exploring every inch that was to be discovered, and I was her guide. I was the one giving her the answers that she wanted, that she needed, in order to open her eyes.

But once her eyes were opened, there was no going back.

"Yes."

The small hint of her smile was just another confirmation that she was it. She was all I needed, all I wanted, all I could ever ask for.

I led her down one of the back paths to a solitary mausoleum. The door was open, as all the others were, and we both stopped at the steps. It was bigger than most of the other buildings, with a double-door entrance, five steps that led to the inside, and a larger frame. Pillars with spiraled ivy lined the front face of the structure, and a faded "A" was engraved at the top. Moss and other plants covered the sides, and grass grew at the bottom.

Celeste glanced to me, then back to the mausoleum. She tilted her head up, looking to the top, causing her hood to slip off her head. Raindrops instantly covered her hair and face, but she didn't seem to notice.

"It's beautiful."

I stood there with my hood still up, the rain dripping off the rim. "It is."

After a moment, Celeste moved forward, away from me. She walked up the first few steps of the mausoleum, leaned down, and placed the carnation on the top landing. The flower, even though it was already wet, rested under the concrete awning and was shielded from the rain. The white and red petals contrasted against the dark cement building, adding a context of color that looked so different from its normal state.

Celeste walked back down and stood beside me, her eyes still glued to the building before her. With her hand stretched out, her palm up, she let the rain fall into her hand. The water ran over her skin, falling to the ground in gravity's pull. I looked over at her, watching as the raindrops slid down her temples, her cheekbones, and down her neck. She looked so ethereal, so intangible, I couldn't wrap my head around it.

But then she turned her head to face me, and I could see why she hid.

Why she hid from me, from the world, from herself.

"Celeste," I pushed my hood down, letting the rain fall on me as well.

She gave me a half smile, as if she knew exactly what I was referring to. My eyes scanned the bright, white shape that lined the left side of her face. It formed a "3", with the top arc running along her hairline, the middle line cutting right under her eyebrow, and the bottom curve resting under her eye, all connected in a single formation.

"It's vitiligo," she stated boldly, not a single quiver in her voice. "It started showing up when I was ten, and I learned to hide it soon after."

"Hide it?" I questioned.

"With makeup."

She lifted the hand that was covered in raindrops, only to show me more white spots on the back of her hand, cleansed from the rainwater.

"It's on my hands and arms, too. It's even on my hairline. I have to get one little section of hair dyed every few weeks. I learned how to hide it all."

With the rainfall continuing to strip away any chance to hide, I continued to stare at her. This was an act of not only vulnerability, but also an invitation to the deepest, most hidden parts of herself.

I have given every part of myself to her, in every aspect, and this was her doing the same. The weight of it was something I could easily recognize.

Narrowing my eyes and brows, I took a single step toward her. "You will never hide yourself from me. Ever. I won't allow it. You understand?"

Her lack of response concerned me for only a moment.

"You will always be the you that I want, no matter how hard you try to cover it up."

She dropped her hand, and her face instantly softened. Streaks of her light brown makeup ran down the sides of her face, blurring away any chance of secrecy in her identity.

"Caius," she began, pushing back at my words. "You don't understand. This isn't something I can simply wash off. People have stared at me. People have laughed at me. I am different, and I am not someone who blends in easily unless I cover myself in my makeup."

I shook my head. "No, I understand all that perfectly. *You're* the one that doesn't understand that I don't give a single *fuck* about any of that. And even though none of that superficial shit matters to me, no one's opinion of you matters except for yours."

Her eyes glazed over with a faint shine as she continued to stare at me.

"I've seen so much death here, *Meum Caelum*. So much grief, so much loss, so much damage. More than you could imagine. And let me tell you, once you're gone, absolutely nothing matters. Not money, not looks, not prized possessions, nothing. We are all reduced to nothing but a single soul."

I lifted my hand to the base of her skull, moving my thumb up to trace the discolored three on her face. I could feel her head tilt into my palm.

"Do not let this be anything more than a piece of your essence. It might define you in your own eyes, but it will *never* define you with me."

Glass shattered on the floor

Burn every paper with the deal

Red water moved in waves

Celeste

Chimes sounded through my car speakers as a phone icon popped up on my car's stereo screen. The name flashed in the space below.

Serena

I tapped the green answer button and put my hand back on the wheel, focusing on the drive ahead of me.

"Hey," I answered.

"Hey, Cel. Sorry I haven't called. I've either been working, sleeping, or everything in between."

I shrugged to myself. "It's no problem. Are you okay?"

"Oh, yeah, I'm fine. I was actually wondering the same thing about you. You freaked me out at Mass."

I scrunched my nose, remembering the way Caius licked the wine off my neck only ten minutes after Serena left. I squeezed my thighs together at the memory of his warm tongue on my skin. "Sorry, I didn't mean to scare you. I just wanted to talk to you about something."

"Okay, what?"

Taking a sharp inhale, I continued to drive as I spoke. "So, you know the place where Uncle Russ is buried?"

Serena paused. "Yeah. What about it?"

"I think…" I started, trying to figure out a way to phase this correctly. "I think Uncle Lucas wants to be buried there, too."

Serena's confusion was bleeding through my car speakers. I could feel it.

"And?" she asked.

"And…" I trailed off, unable to find my wording.

Do I tell her everything? Do I tell her about the Open House? Do I tell her only bits and pieces and leave her to figure it out? Do I brush it all under the rug?

My hands gripped the wheel as I stared at the moving pavement in front of me.

"I don't think it's a good fit for him."

Silence filled the car as I waited for a response.

"What?" Serena finally blurted out.

"I don't think he should be—"

"Why are you concerned with that?" she asked, confusion thick in her tone.

There was no way to answer her without either sounding completely crazy or lying, so I settled with a different reason.

"I don't know why he's even thinking about this now."

"What do you mean, Cel? *Of course,* he's thinking about it. His brother just died. It's probably the *only* thing he's thinking about."

A frustrated groan sat in the bottom of my throat as I let my head tip back, still keeping my eyes on the road.

"I know I'd be the same way if you died," she added.

With the sudden clarity, I wanted to smash my head on the steering wheel. She was so right, and I was so blind, I wanted to take back everything I had already said. My mind has been on Uncle Russ and the things *he* did rather than Uncle Lucas and the things he was going through.

As I turned left onto a hidden street, the trees that lined the road began to look familiar. I knew that if I kept going, it would only be a few more seconds before the call would drop, so I quickly pulled off the side of the road and placed the car in park.

"Sorry, Serena," I exhaled. "I don't know what I was thinking. I just… I don't want to lose anyone else, you know?"

She matched my sigh. "I know. I feel the same way. But you can't let that keep you from living a normal life. Shit happens, and it sucks, but we have to move on."

"You're right," I admitted, letting my hands rest in my lap. I glanced around to the trees and to the bright sunshine peeking through, knowing it was about to fade away and turn to a gloomy rainfall.

"Seriously, Cel, are you okay? You seem like you have a lot going on."

I nodded, even though I knew she couldn't see me. "Yeah, I think I'll be fine. I just need to clear my head and try to *not* think about death for a day."

The words were meant to be lighthearted and sarcastic, but they sounded incredibly real, even to me. I forced the unanticipated feeling away.

"Can you give Nolan a hug for me, please?" I asked before she could call me out on anything else.

"Of course, I can. But you know, you can always come over and give him one yourself."

I released a wide smile, one that felt genuine. "I plan on it. I'll call you soon, okay?"

"Okay. Love you."

"Love you, too."

The call disconnected from the car speakers, leaving the inside silent, and I drove back onto the road. Sure enough, within the next fifty feet, my phone disconnected from any sort of service. The skies began to turn a light grey, and a thin mist lined the pavement. And as I continued on, the rain came, the fog thickened, and the skies darkened.

Here I was, back at Purgatory.

With the rainfall soaking the hood of my jacket, I trotted up the stairs of Caius' house. When I reached the top, I noticed the front door was barely open and unlatched. I narrowed my eyes slightly and decided to push open the door.

"Caius?" My voice echoed in the main corridor with no response.

This is weird. Typically, Caius is always ready for me in every sense.

I stepped completely inside and gently closed the door behind me.

"Ace?"

No answer.

"Mel?"

Still no answer. Ace was around the house far more than Mel was, but it was worth a shot to see if someone was here, especially since the door was open.

Leaving my jacket on, I began to quietly walk down the long, windowed hallway toward Caius' office. Out of all the times I've wandered up to his front door, I've only actually stepped through the threshold twice, and neither one of those times did I go into his office.

Water dripped off my sleeves as I pushed my hood down and untucked my damp hair. The only sound in the whole house was of the raindrops tapping on the glass next to me, and as soothing as it was, I knew something was different.

Not off, but different.

I reached the door to Caius' office and turned the handle. It opened with ease, and I came to see Caius sitting at his desk, with a pen in his hand, his sleeves rolled up, and his hair disheveled. He instantly looked up at me with a blank expression. Across from him, sitting in a lounge chair, was an older woman who had tears sliding down her face.

Oh, *shit.* They were having a meeting.

I think.

I immediately began to step back in shock. "Oh, I am *so* sorry, I didn't mean to—"

Caius interjected. "No. It's fine."

After a quick glance at the woman, my eyes fell over Caius' blank expression as he eased out his words. "Ms. Scott, this is Miss Castell. She and I have a meeting at 3 PM to discuss her future here as well. If it's alright with you, Ms. Scott, I'd prefer she stay."

My eyes volleyed between Caius and Ms. Scott, who agreed to the request. What was he doing? I didn't have a meeting with him, nor did I have an interest in *this* being my final resting point.

With hesitancy, and with a subtle *whatthefuck?* look to Caius, I moved to sit in the other lounge chair that was placed next to the older woman. Hopefully, she wouldn't be appalled at my lack of makeup, revealing the three along the side of my face, or the white roots that I haven't dyed and were beginning to grow as a streak in my hair at the top of my hairline. But reassuringly, she barely paid me any mind as she greeted me with a heavy smile, one that seemed to take too much effort to give.

I looked around the office. It was extremely nice and well put together, but based on the rest of Purgatory, that wasn't surprising. The walls were dark grey, with vibrant green plants in each corner. Windows lined one of the walls, allowing us to see a small section of the grounds through the rain-covered glass. Behind Caius was an unlit fireplace, and on the other wall was a large bookshelf with neatly placed books, binders, and wooden boxes. It was so organized, it looked almost staged, like it was too perfect.

I glanced to the wall behind me to see a monitor split into numerous sections, all showing different areas of the grounds. There were cameras pointing down all the paths, around the house, the greenhouse, and the front gate.

My mind flashed back to when I came here for my uncle's birthday.

Let her in.

He was watching me. It was something I had already assumed, but now had confirmation.

"Ms. Scott was just about to sign her agreement. Right?"

I was pulled back to the conversation just as Ms. Scott nodded, and another tear slipped from her eye. She gave me a side glance and began to explain herself.

"I'm sorry," she started. "It's just been hard for me to think about all of this. I don't want to experience death."

"No one wants to, but everyone does," Caius reassured her, and my eyes flickered over to him. This was a new side to him, one that I'd never seen, nor expected from him. He was being sincere.

Ms. Scott continued. "I know. I wish I had known about this place before my husband died. He would've done this in a heartbeat. And even though we wouldn't have been together, it would've been nice to know he had peace."

Although it was not my place to speak, *at all,* I couldn't help but ask a question. "Why don't you want to be buried with your husband instead of this?"

Caius answered for her. "I offered to exhume her husband, cremate his remains, and place him next to Ms. Scott in the same mausoleum. His spirit may not be signed to Purgatory, but they will be together."

My head tilted only slightly. He was tossing around the word "Purgatory" so loosely, as if it was simply a name. As if it didn't hold significant meaning to every person on Earth. As if it wasn't an end all, be all.

But it was.

This was an extremely heavy decision, and he was sitting here, covering all his bases without a single stutter.

And all I could think about was the fact that my Uncle Russ was once here, sitting in this room, having this same conversation.

Chills immediately ran through my body at the vision.

"That's all I want," Ms. Scott cried softly. "I want to be with him."

"You will," Caius replied, that same empathy still in his tone from earlier. "I'll make sure of it. You have my word."

With her trust in him, Ms. Scott picked up her pen, signed her name at the bottom of the page, and exhaled. Caius took the paper and placed it on top of a manilla folder.

There was a heavy silence in the room as they both paused, anticipating what was next.

"Are you ready?" he asked, and the woman nodded.

I sat in my chair, confused as to what was happening. There was more? Something else was needed besides her signature?

Caius reached into one of his drawers, pulled out an empty vial, and popped the lid off. Along with that, he grabbed a pocketknife and flipped it open, revealing a clean, shiny blade.

My eyes widened at the items.

Oh, fuck. Oh, shit, shit, fuck. I know where this is going.

Caius stood and walked around his desk, making his way between the desk and the woman. After placing a towel on her lap, he leaned back against the wooden frame, and for a split second, my mind wandered. The way the muscles in his arms tightened, the way his chest pressed against his button-down shirt, and the way his large frame was so safe and protective had me trailing out of thought.

But then, when the woman lifted her hand to Caius, and he tenderly grabbed her palm, I was right back to the moment.

She remained sitting as he pressed the knife to her skin and made a diagonal line. Bright red blood instantly pooled in her palm, and her hand cradled the liquid. Caius tilted her hand with the vial underneath and caught most of the blood. A few drops dripped onto the towel, but neither one of them seemed to notice. The vial was about half full before Caius stopped and screwed the lid on.

Then, he reached behind him and grabbed the folder and paper she just signed. He held it to her, presenting it to her, and she looked up at him.

With a slow blink, a nod, and unspoken words, Caius reassured her that she was okay.

Ms. Scott placed her bloody handprint on the paper, sealing herself and her fate, then wrapped her hand in the towel.

Then, Caius surprised me. He kneeled down to Ms. Scott's level and looked her in the eye. There were glistening tears that were teetering over the edge of her eyelids, waiting to fall.

"Ms. Scott," he began, his tone filled with a new compassion. "You will be honored here, as well as your husband. I promise."

She patted his hand and nodded, understanding the decisions that were made. I looked to both of them, vowing internally to never, ever forget this moment.

Celeste

After a few more minutes, Ms. Scott left. Caius ensured she got to her car okay, closed the office door, and locked it. I stood up from the chair, and he looked to me with exhaustion on his face.

"That meeting was not supposed to go past 2:30."

I shook my head. "I'm sorry, I didn't mean to interrupt."

Caius rounded his desk and sorted through the new items from Ms. Scott. He picked up the brand-new vial of blood and walked over to one of the boxes on the bookshelf. Lifting the lid of the box open, he placed the glass in a holder, along with a handful of other vials.

I watched with wide eyes, realizing that all those vials, *that box,* was full of people's blood.

Those were all people who wanted to be here when they died.

There were only about twenty other vials, but as I scanned the rest of the bookshelf, there were probably ten more boxes. There wasn't room for any more, leaving me to wonder if there were more boxes somewhere else.

My chest let out a quiet, quick heave as I realized how *real* this was.

Memories of the first night, the night Caius showed me the ghosts, came back to me.

What I'm about to show you is real.

My heart began to pick up its pace as I silently watched Caius come back to the desk and grab the manilla folder. The paper with the bloody handprint and signature was tucked inside, and Caius took it to a binder on the bookshelf. Once again, there were hundreds of other folders and papers, signifying the agreement of the others.

And my Uncle Russ was mixed in there, somewhere.

His bloody handprint.

His scribbled signature.

Did he hesitate? Did he sign with a smile? Did he think of his brothers, his family? Did he ever think I would find out?

"Celeste?" Caius asked, snapping me out of my questions. He was standing back at his desk, his hair mussed, his hands in his pockets. My eyes met his stare, confusion over multiple things settling between us.

"Was he happy?" I finally managed to ask.

"Who?"

"My uncle."

Caius nodded once, as if he was expecting this conversation at some point. With a minor uncertainty in his body language, I could see him processing his answer before saying it. The muscles in his inked forearms flexed, traveling up the length of his arms and reaching his shoulders.

"Yes. He was."

Without being able to stop myself, I blurted out my next thought. "I want to do it."

Caius immediately froze. "Do what?"

"I want to do it. I want to see what it was like for him. I want to sign it."

Caius' silver irises flared, a sudden fury lighting his face. "Absolutely not."

"Yes," I argued. "Let me sign it. Give me a knife."

Caius held firm and shook his head. "Celeste, no. This isn't you. This is your grief talking."

"No, it's not," I bit back. "Don't talk about my grief, and don't tell me what I can and can't do. Give me the paper." I remained on my feet, my eyes still meeting his, my stance firm.

"No." His voice was strong, stronger than it had ever been with me before.

I wasted no time in coming around to his side of the desk. I began opening drawers one by one, my hands filtering through the material in them, only to feel Caius' arms wrap around me and attempt to pull me away. I tried to cling to the wooden frame, my hands grabbing the drawers, the lip of the desk, *anything,* but my efforts were futile.

"Caius, let me go. Give me the paper, and let me *go.* "

My voice cracked on the last word as a sudden sadness filled my chest, but I still managed to keep up my fight against his hold. I kicked my feet out as he lifted me off the ground and stepped backward, away from the desk. I could feel his legs back into the grated cover of the fireplace, causing it to rattle behind us.

"Put me down," I demanded through clenched teeth. *"Now!"* I could hear myself turning needy, and I couldn't help the emotion that was flooding into my words.

"No." His voice was calm, firm, and steady. His grip on me was effortless, and my squirming was doing nothing in my favor. "I can't let you."

"I need to know, Caius, please." I could begin to feel my eyes well up with tears. I blinked up to the ceiling, trying to keep the sorrow locked inside. My breathing was heavy, not only from the restraint, but also from the fact that Caius was right.

I was still so *fucking* sad.

Every new chapter here was a new chapter in my grief. Everything I learned about this, about my uncle, had the healing wound opening again. And there was nothing I could do to stop it.

"Please," I whispered, his arms still locking me in place. "I just want to see what it was like for him."

A single tear spilled out and ran down my cheek. My pulse felt as if it was about to explode out of my chest as I tried to calm down. I could feel the strong arms around me hesitate in the tight grasp, but soon he gave me a squeeze, then relented and let me go.

"Sit," he commanded, and I obeyed. I walked back to the lounge chair I was in before and sat down.

"Other one," he motioned to the chair next to me, and I glanced over to it. "He was sitting in that chair."

I swallowed the ache in my throat and moved over, relishing in the intricate detail. My hands rested on the velvet armrests, and the feeling hit me all over again.

He was here.

Caius' eyes pierced through mine with a depth so significant, it felt dangerous.

"There's nothing I want more than for you to be mine for the rest of time. I'd give everything for you, to be with you, and to have you. But you deserve more than just me, *Meum Caelum,* and if you think I'm going to let you sign your soul to me, to *this,* you're out of your fucking mind."

Caius moved to sit at his usual spot at his desk. Reaching down, he opened one of the drawers and pulled out a white paper. He placed it on the surface of the desk and slid it over to me.

My wet, glossy eyes unlocked from his and moved down to the paper. With words that were too blurred for my eyes to read, there was a decent-sized paragraph and a signature line toward the bottom, but other than that, the page was blank.

But this was the page that everyone had been presented with. This was the page Ms. Scott just signed, that my uncle signed before he died, and that my other uncle is considering signing.

"Give me a pen," I spoke, straightening my spine.

"Celeste," Caius growled, and I shook my head.

"I'm not going to give you my blood. I just want to sign it."

With a deep groan, Caius handed over a pen. I took it, uncapped it, and signed my name on the bottom of the page.

I wanted to feel what it felt like to promise myself to something else, something that I didn't have the answers to until recently. It was a strange sight, seeing my name scribbled in ink on a page that determined where I would be for the rest of eternity.

But at the same time, I couldn't feel anything at all. Maybe it was because I wasn't fully committed, and I had no desire to be. At least, not anytime soon.

Maybe it was different for my uncle because he knew he didn't have much time left.

Then again, does anyone *really* know when it's time?

I tilted my head at the paper as an idea struck me. *Maybe I should sign over everything completely.*

As if Caius was reading my thoughts, he voiced his concern. "Don't even think about it."

I looked up at him, and his intense stare fixed on mine.

"In order for the agreement to work, an entire handprint is needed," he explained. "But I don't want a single *fucking* drop of your blood on that page, so don't even think about it."

My curiosity got the best of me as I asked, "Why don't you want me here?"

Caius' jaw ticked at my question. He rested his forearms on the desk and leaned forward. "Did you hear me, Celeste? There's nothing I want more than to keep you. Every piece of my soul is connected to you, intertwined with you, always, in every moment. My soul is yours, my body is yours. Every breath I take is yours. For you, and only you. I want all of you to myself."

I watched as he momentarily wavered and broke his gaze with me.

"But you, your body and soul are bigger than this could ever be. Your essence exceeds anything this place has to offer. If there's something better out there, I will never deprive you of it. You deserve more than this."

A sudden ache in my chest bloomed. There has never been anyone besides my family that has viewed me as something worth more than an ordinary life. I have never felt that worthiness in such a drastic way, and his words made my soul swell. He was shielding me from Purgatory by directing me to Heaven. He was, in an odd way, protecting me from the mundane and offering me to Paradise.

"You will not commit to this. Understood?"

I could do nothing but nod in agreement. After all, I wasn't ready to promise myself yet—if ever—so I had no problem with his demand.

"Did he say anything?" I muttered, changing the topic as I slid the bloodless paper back to him.

Caius shook his head, understanding who I was referring to. "No. It was all business."

"He didn't say anything about me? About his family?"

Caius let out a sympathetic sigh. "No."

"And you don't know why he chose this? Over the chance that he could go to Heaven?" My bottom lip began to quiver, so I quickly pulled it in between my teeth and bit down, trying to suppress my rampant emotions.

"Do you know what he did for a living, Caius?" I asked but didn't give him space to answer. "He was a surgeon. He saved people's lives every day. He did *heart transplants.*"

Caius took notice of my sentiments and stood up, walked to my chair, and kneeled down in front of me.

"He was a good person," I continued, my own perception of my uncle stated as matter-of-fact. "Why did he choose this?"

He reached up and traced the exposed, uncovered three on my face with his thumb. "If I knew his train of thought, I would tell you. But I don't, and I'm sorry for that."

His sincerity was shining through again, and the tone warmed me. He was being honest, I could see it in him, and there was no way I could fault him for that.

And like a lot of people in this world, I lost someone without knowing all the answers. I will never understand why he made the decisions he did, and I have to accept that.

With a sigh, my hand moved up to rest over top of his, the warmth of him cradled under my palm. I didn't want to think about any of it anymore. I was done asking questions, and I was done trying to fill in the blanks for others.

I did not expect to come here today and experience these emotions, but I'm glad I did. I had to get them out somehow, in some way, and I'm thankful Caius was here to help me.

Week after week, I would show up to my uncle's mausoleum every Thursday to visit. It was the same thing every time: the small building in pristine condition, the sorrow I felt at the absence of his presence, and the rain that washed away my insecurities.

Most of the time, Caius would meet me inside the mausoleum to take me. To strip me down to nothing, to feel my skin on his, and to join us as one.

And sometimes, I would find myself wandering up to his front door, wanting to see him *before* feeling that grief. I wanted my body to feel the pleasure he gave me before it felt the sorrow buried inside. He would meet me at the door and guide me to the hidden room in the greenhouse, where he would then take me, claim me.

Then, I began to show up on Sundays after Mass, because the words and teachings there had my head confused, and I needed clarity in Purgatory. And then I started to visit on Tuesdays after work, just because it was convenient.

And then… I showed up whenever I felt like it. With no justification needed.

But in my visits, I still protected myself. I was always gone and home before sundown.

In a sense, Caius helped me heal. His distraction from the loss pushed me into a healthier state of mind, one that looked at the death in a different light.

Uncle Russ was gone, but in that inevitable fact, he got to choose his next life.

Somewhere along those lines, I couldn't help it. Things were switching for me.

My views, my opinions, my outlook.

One year ago, I would've never agreed with any of this. I would've laughed, rolled my eyes, whatever. But now that I've seen the love behind it all, the freedom it gives to those who fear the afterlife, and the power in peace, there's a part of me that will always stand behind it.

But a small, nagging part of me will always wonder what else is out there.

If there's Purgatory, then of course there's Hell.

But there's also Heaven.

And wouldn't that be better than this?

Ace met me at the front door the second I stepped inside. "Hey," he whispered, his hand to his lips. "Caius is with someone."

"Another meeting?" I asked, matching his hushed tone. "Didn't he just have one yesterday?"

Caius' meetings were not frequent, but they happened often enough to keep the business afloat. The fact that he was cooped up in his office two days in a row was definitely out of the ordinary.

Ace shook his head, his blonde hair shifting slightly along the top of his forehead. "I don't think this is a meeting. More like an offer."

I narrowed my eyes. Someone else wanted to own Purgatory. I'm sure the offer was a good one, since the weight of the ownership was heavy.

"Caius will tell him to fuck off. He always does." Ace shut the door behind me, clicking it in place. "Give it ten minutes, maybe less."

"Where's Mel?" I asked, keeping my voice low.

"She's on a date with that Ethan guy."

"Ethan?"

"Yeah, Ethan Vail." Ace started, shoving his hands in his pockets. "A guy she's been seeing off and on for a while now. He's a total jackass, but I don't know. There's something in him she likes." Ace's eyes fell to the red box in my hands. "Whatcha got there?"

I grinned and handed him the box, allowing me to take off my rain jacket. "It's a surprise."

"Surprise, huh?" Ace smiled back. He was dressed casually, wearing a grey band t-shirt and dark blue jeans.

Once my jacket was off and hung up, I took the box back and made my way to the kitchen, with Ace following close behind. I placed the box on the center island counter, opened it, and sat down on one of the island's stools.

"Those smell so good," Ace remarked, sitting down on a stool next to mine. He leaned in to peek into the box. "What are they?"

"They're Red Panda cookies," I began as Ace reached in and took one out. "They're from The Red Panda Bakery. My mom used to work there before she got pregnant with Serena, and since then, we've been going there almost every week. Sometimes more. It's a local business not too far from here, and sometimes they struggle to stay open, so I do my best to buy from them when I can."

I reached in and grabbed a cookie, my mouth watering at the simple sight of it.

"They're just red velvet cookies with white chocolate chips, but their recipe is amazing. I don't know what they put in them. My mom knows, but she refuses to tell me. Whatever it is, it's so good, and they've won awards to prove it."

Ace took a bite, and his eyes went wide. I could see the enjoyment in his expression as he continued to chew.

"Holy shit, Cel, these are amazing."

I flashed a smirk, taking a bite of my own cookie, my heart warming a bit at the mention of Ace using my nickname. Not only was I becoming more comfortable with myself, with this place, and with everyone else, but they were also comfortable with me.

The first time I came here without my makeup on, to say I was nervous would be an understatement. My palms were sweaty, and my heart was racing, all at the chance that someone would see me and think differently of me. I was afraid they would see the three on my skin, see the growing white streak on my hairline, and laugh at me.

But when I stepped in that door, with Ace and Mel in the main corridor, they treated me as if nothing was different. They didn't say anything, they didn't point it out, and I don't think they even looked at it for more than a second. I don't know if Caius had a hand in that, but if he did, I was thankful.

I wanted to be treated like everyone else, and them not saying anything made me feel like there was nothing different about me.

I was grateful.

Now, as I sat across from Ace as we ate our cookies, I felt like I had somewhere I could be myself completely.

Somewhere I belonged.

"I can't remember the last time I saw Caius eat a cookie," Ace stated, his mouth full of the red treat. "Mel usually makes Christmas cookies every year, so maybe then? But she was sick last Christmas, so, two years ago?" he mumbled to himself, clearly thinking out loud.

His thoughts triggered a question in me.

"Have you and Mel lived here long?"

Ace swallowed the rest of his mouthful and brushed any crumbs off his hands. "Yeah," he replied, furrowing his brows slightly. "Cai didn't tell you?"

I shook my head. "I never asked."

Ace nodded. "Mel and I were foster kids our whole lives. We bounced from home to home until we were almost eight, and that's when the Attilas adopted us."

I put my half-eaten cookie on the counter. "So, you came here when you were eight?" I verified. "Weren't you scared of all this?"

Ace grinned. "Shitless."

That made me return the smile, but only for a moment as he elaborated.

"Seeing everything that goes on here at night really, *really* scared me at first. But Mr. and Mrs. Attila kept telling me and Mel that the spirits were harmless, they couldn't hurt us, things like that.

They would sit with me whenever I got scared. They were parents first, and they took that role very seriously."

My heart pattered at the thought of Ace and Mel as young kids, scared by all their new surroundings, constantly given comfort whenever they needed it.

"Even Cai would try to make Mel and me feel better. He would go out during the night, stand out in the path while we watched from the window, all to show us there was nothing to be afraid of. And it worked. After a while, we became used to it, and now it's normal to us."

I rested my elbow on the counter as I listened, propping my chin in the palm of my hand.

"I'm thankful for him. He's our brother."

My heart doubled in size at Ace's words, and my pulse made it feel like it was about to burst from behind my ribcage. There were no words to explain how I felt for Caius, and hearing Ace's story simply verified my feelings. Caius was honest, he was comforting, and he was supportive. He was strong, he was firm, and he had his head on straight.

Every part of my body warmed in a tingle that felt never-ending.

Ace sighed. "Which is why it's so fucked that Dey is the way he is. It's one thing to not believe in this, but it's another to actively try to take it down. His family, Mel and I included, did nothing but *be a family*. He's lucky he had good parents and siblings who always loved him."

"Were you close with him?"

He nodded. "Yeah. Until he left."

His statement was so short and so abrupt that I knew he didn't want to talk about it. He had no desire to relive the memory, so I didn't press any further.

I broke off a piece of cookie and popped it in my mouth, savoring the sweet, rich flavor. Ace reached into the box for another one.

"You know," he started after taking another bite. "I've never seen Caius like this."

"Like what?"

Ace stopped his chewing to send me a knowing look. The corners of his mouth lifted slightly, and he tilted his head toward me. "You know."

A set of butterflies released in the pit of my stomach. I *did* know, but having someone else notice it, too, had me floating.

"I've known him for most of my life. I grew up with him. I've been there with him through everything."

I picked at the last piece of cookie that rested on the counter, my eyes falling to the unpigmented spots on the back of my hand.

"He's different now, in a good way. *You* brought that out of him."

My eyes met Ace's, and his kindness and affection practically spilled out of him.

"He brought that out of me, too."

Footsteps sounded in the hall outside of the kitchen, and soon enough, Caius stepped through the open frame. My heart skipped at the sight of him, with his usual white button down, unbuttoned at the top to show his inked chest, and the sleeves rolled to the elbows, presenting thick, tattooed arms. With his heated, grey-eyed stare on me, he slowly wandered over, his steps easy and his stride smooth. Approaching me, I found myself silently holding my breath as his body leaned in close, his eyes never breaking his gaze with mine. Without saying a word, his body brushed against my knees as he angled himself forward and grabbed a cookie from the box beside me.

Celeste

Plopping down in the sand, I pushed my bare toes under the cool, smooth surface. Caius did the same, with his legs bent and his inked forearms draped over his knees. I loved seeing him in a natural setting, since he hardly ever stepped off the grounds of Purgatory. Even though his body remained tense, I could see a subtle relaxation forming in his posture.

"So, an offer, huh?" I asked as we settled, my white zip-up sweatshirt slipping off one of my shoulders.

Caius brushed some sand off the backs of his khaki pants. "A shitty one," he replied.

"What do you mean?"

He gave a half shrug. "It just wasn't anything worth my time."

I looked over to him, studying the profile that I've come to memorize. "Are *any* of the offers worth your time?"

The muscle in Caius' jaw tensed as he glanced to me, then back to the scene in front of him. "No."

That was one of the many things I admired about him. He was so sure of himself, of everything in his life, and he had no time for bullshit.

But he had time for me.

And he had time to sit with me on the beach.

"When's the last time you've been here?" I asked, gently nudging him with my shoulder.

Caius moved his hand up to his jaw, tenderly brushing his fingers against the dark stubble. "It's been a long time."

"And when's the last time you've seen a sunset?" I asked. "A *real,* cloudless, rainless sunset?"

A long, heavy pause weighted itself between us.

"Even longer."

Even though I knew Caius didn't mind it, my heart cracked at the monotony of his life.

Caius glanced back over to me briefly, and I could see his eyes fall down to my exposed shoulder. I watched as his gaze traced the tan line that ran across my skin, and I knew exactly what he was thinking.

My darkening skin saw the sun long enough to change its color. It was from the same sun that never showed its face in Purgatory.

My *life* saw the sun. A life that would never see the sun if I committed myself to Purgatory.

Part of me understood where Caius was coming from. If I were in his shoes, I would understand it even more.

But that didn't stop me from disagreeing with him and his stance on me.

We both sat in the sand, watching as the sky slowly turned from blue, to red and pink, then to a deep shade of indigo. The blood-orange sun rested just above the horizon, easing its descension into nightfall. Rippling waves washed up onto the shore, creating an echoing soundtrack in the space around us.

"I want you to know, Celeste," Caius began, breaking the silence and keeping his gaze on the sunset. "I'll give you everything you want. Anything, it's yours."

I tore my eyes away from the beautiful colors in the sky to look at him. His face was tight, his expression was stoic, and I knew he was fighting something internally.

"And what if I only want you?"

Caius didn't answer. There were probably a thousand thoughts treading through his mind, just like mine, and the ability to organize and silence them was pointless.

I didn't want to think about the sand that was sure to be stuck to our feet as we made our way back to the car. I didn't want to think about the ghosts we were going to see when we made it back to Purgatory. I didn't want to think about the paper in Caius' office that had my name, but didn't have my blood.

So instead of talking, instead of focusing on the things we couldn't change, we watched as the final sliver of sun faded into the depths of twilight, simply enjoying each other's presence. Because, in that moment, that's all we had.

Caius drove us back up the hills to Purgatory, his hand gripping the inside of my thigh the entire way. Without even blinking, he took the fogged turns with ease, not a single bit of hesitation in his drive. He had the path memorized from top to bottom, while every time I made the drive, I was still slipping off the road once in a while.

The road was still wet from the day's rain as we approached the gate.

Lawrence greeted us from his usual post. "Good evening, Mr. Attila, Miss Castell."

"Hi, Lawrence!" I shouted through the driver's window, which Caius rolled down halfway.

"Everything okay?" Caius asked.

"Everything's as good as can be, Mr. Attila."

Lawrence gave a tip of his chin as he opened the entrance.

With the separation of the ivy-covered gates, my breath caught in my throat. The headlights from the car illuminated the spirits ahead, just like the first night I saw them. Despite the blinding lights, they continued to walk aimlessly along the paths, wondering in the space given. Their steps were leisurely, calm, and casual.

Caius could immediately sense my unease. With his hand still gripping the inside of my thigh, he gave me a reassuring squeeze, making his solace known.

I closed my eyes. If anyone could drive through the spirits, it's him.

"Hey," he spoke with a gentleness. "I got you. Don't be afraid."

Forcing myself to take his words to heart, I opened my eyes. The car made its way through the path, passing the giant statue of the Angel of Grief, stopping intermittently between ghosts. All of them kept their focus on the path ahead, and none of them cared about us. They were in their own version of their afterlife, with nothing to focus on but themselves.

By the time we made it to the house, my anxiety was still high, but it was manageable. I was still scared, and I knew it was something I couldn't change right away, but at least I was facing it head-on.

Caius got out of the car, made his way to my side, and opened my door for me. I climbed out, the damp air refreshing my skin as I breathed it in.

And as soon as my foot hit the pavement, I looked up to meet the stare of my Uncle Russ.

My heart fell into the pit of my stomach as he continued to walk toward me, but off to the side a bit. He was following the path in front of the house, his steps carrying him in a stride I've known my whole life.

Within seconds, he passed me, nearly brushing my shoulder as he didn't break pace.

I remained frozen in place, unable to move anything besides my eyes as I watched him go. Once he was a few feet down the path, I turned and looked over my shoulder, watching him as the shadows swallowed his spirit whole.

Everything in me was telling me to go. I needed to take off and get out of here because this is against everything I've come to know in my entire life.

But the second my body moved to run, a strong arm wrapped around my body, lifting me back against his warmth. I panicked and kicked out my legs in an attempt to flee from the haunted grounds.

Caius held me close to him, not in a capture, but more as a safety net.

Breathe, Celeste. Breathe.

It's him, but it's not him anymore.

I did my best to calm my racing heart as Caius moved his hand up to the side of my face, brushing my hair away.

"Stay with me," he hushed, his words dark and soft.

And I knew that if I wanted to be with him, I had to face my fears.

Black silk sheets wrapped around me as my body stirred, slowly waking to the dim dawn filtering through the windows. I reached over to the other side of the bed, hoping to feel the one person I wanted, only to be met with cool material under my touch. I peeked one eye open to confirm my suspicions. Caius was gone.

The silk felt so good against my bare body, but I needed to know where he went. Slowly climbing out of bed, I searched for my clothes, only to find them sporadically thrown throughout the room. I could feel my face turn a deep shade of red at the memory of him ripping my clothes off and throwing me onto the bed, leaving no part of my skin untouched.

Instead of trotting around and trying to collect my clothes, I tiptoed into the master bathroom to pee. Then, I grabbed the black cotton robe that hung on the wall of the shower and put it on, the fabric instantly warming me. I rinsed my mouth with mouthwash as a temporary fix until I could find Caius to ask for a spare toothbrush.

Judging by the limited light coming in from the window, I knew dawn was just around the corner, but Caius didn't have any clocks around to confirm.

Did clocks even work around here?

Stepping out of the bathroom, I could see a sliver of a black pantleg on the balcony. I walked over and quietly opened the door to see Caius sitting outside, his legs spread as he leaned back in his chair.

Morning Caius was a sight I didn't know I needed to see until now. With his black sweatpants, he wore a loose, grey sweatshirt, and his messy, dark hair stuck out in the most random places. His eyes were alert but still sleepy as he looked to me, his index finger brushing against his lower lip. I smiled wide, loving this unknown side of him.

"Can't sleep?" he asked.

"My shifts at the coffee shop start pretty early, so I'm used to it." I stepped toward the railing, cautiously looking down to the populated paths below. "But I should be asking *you* that question," I added, throwing a quick glance to him over my shoulder.

There was a brief silence between us, one that I didn't know was there until he spoke again. "No one has ever spent the night before."

And with those words out in the open, I turned myself back to him. His grey eyes held vulnerability, revealing a fact that meant more than what was simply spoken.

He never had someone sleep in his bed overnight before. Whether that was by choice or not didn't matter. This was different. This was new to him. Not only did he let me into the secrets of Purgatory, but he also let me into the simplicities of *his life.*

Our eyes held a stare for a moment before he quickly stood to his feet, closed the space between us, and kissed me. His hand found the back of my neck, threading itself through my hair as his lips pushed against mine, needing me. Aching for me.

Breaking the kiss, he pressed his forehead to mine, keeping his eyes closed.

"You wanted me to see the sunset," he began, his words warm against my lips. "But what about the sunrise?" he asked, finally opening his eyes. Caius gently turned my body so I was looking back over the railing, his front flush with my back.

Daylight was starting to find its way above the horizon. Although the skies were still filled with gloom, they turned from a darkened black, to a charcoal, then finally to the slate grey I've become accustomed to.

I watched as the lingering spirits made their way through the paths, slowly dissipating as day approached. One by one, they found their mausoleums and stepped inside, vanishing until the next nightfall.

That's why all the doors were open- so they could leave at night and return in the morning.

My eyes scanned the grounds until I found my uncle's mausoleum. I could only see part of the side, but I knew it was his, even from a distance. I kept my eyes there for minutes, waiting to see him again.

And sure enough, with the sun rays lightening the clouded skies, I watched as he strolled back to his mausoleum, took the three steps up, and disappeared inside.

My body felt stuck as I remained rooted to the spot. I was torn. Half of me knew this was what he wanted; that was obvious, but the other half didn't have the answer to why, and that absence of information couldn't connect the dots.

But he was resting. He was at peace.

And with Caius' arms around me, I inhaled the damp air as the rain began again. At first, it came in tiny droplets, then it formed into a steady fall. Caius grabbed my hand and pulled me back inside before we got too wet.

Between last night's sunset and this morning's sunrise, I knew I would never look at life the same.

Caius

Peering out through my second-floor window, I watched as Celeste drove her car up to the house. She parked right outside of the front door, got out, and locked it behind her. For a few weeks now, she hasn't been bothering to see her uncle first. She comes straight to me.

I'd be lying if I said that didn't set something off in me. I could feel my muscles tensing at the thought of her touch, and my already half-hard cock twitched at the idea of her body needing *me* before anything else.

But a small sliver of myself felt some sort of guilt, which felt foreign. Usually, I'm good at dissociating myself away from feelings and emotions, so the fact that I wanted her to *feel* better, not just act as if she was, was new to me.

But I know how this goes. I've seen it time and time again—the layers of grief that never truly go away until time has healed them. And although everyone is different, I know that it is *never* an easy path.

I could hear the front door open below. The fact that she's comfortable enough to walk in the house without knocking, without waiting to be invited in, speaks volumes.

And it was like a light had been switched on in me.

Heading out of my bedroom in grey sweatpants and a white t-shirt, I made my way down the left set of stairs and moved to the main staircase. Celeste was nowhere to be seen, but after a brief moment of silence, I could hear laughter coming from the kitchen.

Once I entered the hallway under the stairs, I could instantly smell something amazing. My mouth began to water at the delectable smell, and I had a hunch that Celeste followed it, too.

As I finally reached the kitchen, my eyes scanned the room. Ace sat on one of the stools along the far end of the broad center island, leaning over a plate full of food and taking a bite. Mel stood at the stove, stirring whatever smelled good in the pot in front of her. And, sure enough, there stood Celeste at the near side of the island, with her elbows propped up on the countertop and her ass barely resting on a bar stool. She wore jeans and a tight brown sweater, which complimented her curves beautifully. Her dark brown hair fell in waves past her shoulders, with half of it pulled back and away from her face. From the doorway, I watched as she smiled at something Ace said, and her expression lit up the entire fucking room.

Fuck.

Something struck a chord in me, something that I didn't know I could feel.

"Hey, Cai," Ace greeted me with a mouthful of food, acknowledging me as I remained in the doorway.

Celeste turned to face me, and my chest instantly began to swell.

She was barely wearing any makeup. Her three was prominently visible, and yet she still had a smile on her face.

She was comfortable not only with me but also with Ace and Mel. Her whole life, she spent hiding from herself and everyone around her, until now. Either I unlocked something free in her, or maybe Purgatory did, or maybe it was a combination of both.

Whatever it was, it had me rubbing the back of my neck, a drop of unease in a sea of satisfaction.

"You hungry?" Ace asked. Without saying anything, I shook my head, and Celeste looked at me, suddenly puzzled. Her eyebrows narrowed in confusion as she sat up straighter and tilted her head.

Mel exhaled a laugh as she moved away from the stove and squeezed a lemon wedge into her drink. "Nope. He doesn't get any if he's going to pout like that."

Ace shot her a look, one that she instantly returned. I knew they were speaking their thoughts to each other in their minds, which was something they'd always been good at. It's their stupid fucking twin telepathy, and I quickly learned to dismiss it whenever I saw it.

Celeste slid off her stool and took a step toward me. "You okay?" she asked, her tone hushed.

My eyes met hers, the golden-brown shimmering irises lighting up with each and every blink. God, I was more than fucking okay, but my natural tendencies were beginning to push through.

With a quick glance to the others, I leaned forward slightly. "Come with me," I commanded, letting my hands fall back into my pockets. Without waiting for an answer, I turned to go, and I could hear Celeste's footsteps follow. I guided her up the stairs and to the left, leading her to the last door in the hallway.

She has been here before, once on the night of the Open House party, and again just a few nights ago when she slept in my bed. *My bed,* the one that has always been just mine and has never been slept in by anyone other than me.

I pushed open the door to my bedroom, a light scent of sandalwood and earth tones wafting in our direction. Celeste stepped through the threshold, and I gently closed the door behind her.

"What's going on?" she asked with a hint of worry.

A small piece of me broke as I heard the faint quiver in her voice, and I knew I had to ease it away completely.

"Fuck. I don't know what it is, Celeste." I ran a hand through my dark hair, gently pulling at the roots.

"Caius?"

I didn't give her any more room to speak. "I've always been reserved and closed off, I guess it's just from the way the world works here. I've avoided attachment to everything because I know that death is inevitable. But now that I see you with this," I reached up and brushed the three with my fingertips, "and I see how comfortable you are here, I know, with absolutely no doubt in my mind, that you fit here. I'll never try to convince you to believe in this, or to commit your soul to me. Even if that's what you want to do, that's not my intention. But with every passing moment with you, I just know. You belong in this world, *with me,* and that scares the living fuck out of me because no one has ever belonged here like you do."

Her eyes glistened in the gloomy daylight as she soaked in my words, her face soft and gentle.

"There has *never* been anyone like you, Celeste, and there will never be anyone but you."

I watched as her throat moved in a swallow, pushing down all the emotion I was giving to her. And, with a straightforward step, she closed the space between us, reached up on her toes, and pressed her lips onto mine. It was the sweetest taste, the richest touch, and I had it right here, in the afterworld between Heaven and Hell.

My hands instinctively picked her up from under her thighs, causing her to wrap herself around me. I walked her across the room to the bed and laid her down, her dark hair fanning out under her, contrasting the pure white silk sheets. Her hands immediately undid her jeans, and she pushed them down and off her legs. I helped her take off her sweater, leaving her bare to me. The backs of her hands, the bends of her elbows, and the bottoms of her collarbones were all depigmented from her vitiligo, and this was the first time I could truly acknowledge that she wasn't trying to cover herself from me.

There was no hiding. There was no running.

This was her, exposing all of herself to me, in the most vulnerable of ways.

Reaching down, I took both of her hands and kissed my way up her arms, marking every inch of her skin, vitiligo or not. There was nothing I didn't want from her.

When my lips found their way to the top of her shoulder, I paused to grip my shirt at the back of my neck and pull it off, only tearing myself away from her for a second. I kicked off my sweatpants and boxer briefs, leaving me just as bare as her.

My lips kissed her neck, nipping and sucking interchangeably as slight moans slipped from her tongue. It was taking all of me to soak her in, to devour her slowly, rather than giving in and rushing my way into her.

But with every groan, with every arch of her back and claw in my skin, I drove closer and closer to simply easing my way into her without a second thought.

My hand grasped the back of her neck as my thumb stroked her jawbone. I could feel her goosebumps under me as our bodies rested against one another, our skin connecting in a desired heat.

"Caius," she echoed to me, knowing that my name on her tongue is my ultimate weakness. It was her way of claiming me, even though my soul was already eternally promised to her.

"Fuck, Meum Caelum, I'm not even inside you yet, and I already feel as if I could release everything to you."

She hummed her approval through closed lips, a gentle grin settling in her expression. I leaned up and kissed the three that lined the left side of her face, letting my hair fall down over my forehead and barely over my closed eyes.

My free hand moved down Celeste's body, brushing against every goosebump I could find. My fingertips trailed down over her hipbone, releasing a shutter that racked through her body. Her sensitive skin quivered under my touch as I moved to the space between her legs, letting my hands feel the radiating warmth she had for me.

My lips remained against the side of her face as my fingers slid into her pussy, her arousal instantly soaking me and making my cock twitch. Fuck, I didn't think I could get any harder, but she was proving me wrong by simply existing.

With a sharp inhale, Celeste bit her bottom lip at my fingers' pleasure. I swirled them around, letting her walls grip me with each motion. My thumb moved up to her clit, mirroring the same act as my other fingers. Her hands grabbed my arm, her fingertips digging into my flesh as hard as they could. Her breath was beginning to quicken as my actions increased in intensity. From the corner of my eyes, I watched as her chest heaved and her legs squirmed.

"Caius, *please,*" she begged, her voice, her body, her soul aching for me.

My fingers ripped out of her, leaving her to wallow in their absence. After quickly bringing them to my lips and licking her off of them, my hand moved down to fist my throbbing cock. It pulsed in my hand as I stroked it slowly, lining it up at her swollen entrance.

"I will be the only one for you, Celeste. Forever. I will be the only one to be inside you, from now until the end of eternity."

With that, I slammed into her, our hipbones meeting in a shocked connection. Celeste let out an ethereal cry, one that could be heard from the mountains of the Heavens above and the valleys of Hell below.

And here we are, in the Between, in our own little pocket of this realm. Just her and I, as one.

My hand found its way to her throat as I caressed the light brown skin. Her scent was filling my lungs as I breathed her in, not letting her away from me for a single second.

I continued to thrust into her, my dick hitting every inch of her insides as I released a deep rumble of a growl. Her pussy felt so tight, so fucking gripped, and I knew there was no way I could last much longer.

Her legs hooked under my thighs, allowing me to shift deeper inside of her, creating friction on our skin.

"Fucking Hell, baby," I said through a clenched jaw, shaking my head. "I'm so fucked."

I meant it in the best way possible. There was nothing like this, like her, and I could feel her attachment in my bones.

And I knew it from the first second I saw her.

She smiled in satisfaction as her hands ran through my hair, her nails gently scraping my scalp, creating a new form of ecstasy coursing through my veins.

With each thrust, her body became more and more stiff, and I knew she was on the cusp. I slammed myself into her again, and that's when she cried out to me, her back arched and her legs squeezing me. I followed her over the edge, my own body convulsing as I released everything into her, leaving nothing unfinished.

Her lips found mine again in an act of comfort, one that couldn't be duplicated by anything else.

And the train of thought was simple- everything came back down to her.

The pleasure of her and I together was something I knew I could no longer live without.

Celeste

My fingertips rested under the stream of the faucet. The water was on the hotter side, just as I liked it. I pulled my hair up into a messy bun, letting stray locks of hair fall out in waves.

"I have something for you," Caius rumbled in my ear. I remained sitting on the edge of the bathtub as he left my back, leaving my bare skin cold. He reached down into a cabinet under the sink and pulled out a small plastic bag.

"What is that?" I asked.

"You'll see," he replied with a grin. "Get in."

Obeying his command, I turned off the running water and slid my body down into the tub. It took a second to get used to the heat, but once I was in, I was fine. Caius waited outside the bath with a subtle grin, still naked, as he watched me get settled. A light layer of white foam surrounded me, clinging to me as I turned and glanced to Caius. He reached into the bag, pulled out a handful of flower petals, and scattered them over the water's surface.

Bringing my hand up from the water, I grabbed one.

They were carnation petals. Small and silky, white with a red outline.

The same flowers from the first time Caius and I ever spoke.

Once he was done, he placed the empty bag on the counter and returned to the tub. Without hesitation, he climbed into the tub with me, causing the water to rise up to my collarbones. He nestled in behind me, situating himself so my body was cradled between his legs. My back rested against his chest as I exhaled a new, comfortable relief.

His arms wrapped around my front as his cheek rested against the side of my head.

"What are you thinking about?" he asked.

Moving my gaze up to the window, I watched as steady streams of rainfall streaked down the glass. A green hue filtered in from the wet, heavy foliage, creating a natural, earthy atmosphere, and I relaxed in the ambiance.

"How this bathtub is my favorite part of the whole house," I said with a small laugh, and I could feel him smile behind me. "And how I don't want to leave," I added, my fingers swirling in the hot water around me.

"Then don't," Caius whispered, and I could feel my insides flutter. His lips moved down to my shoulder as he kissed the skin delicately.

I blinked away the blunt reply and pictured it myself, in my own mind.

I could see us, wrapped up in his silk sheets, listening to the rainfall patter on the roof above us. The spirits would surround us every night as we entwined our bodies, focusing on nothing or no one else but ourselves.

A hint of a smile grew on my lips as I became fond of the idea.

But then I thought of reality, and how simply staying wasn't anything more than a dream.

"I can't," I rasped, letting the flower petals slide between my fingers, even though I desperately wanted to stay.

His lips moved up to my neck, and I tilted my head away to give him better access to my skin. "Why not?" he asked, then didn't give me a chance to answer. "I will give you everything you need. Anything you want, it's yours."

"And if I want to be *here,* forever?"

His kisses stilled, understanding my implication.

I wanted my soul to be tied to Purgatory.

"No."

I could feel his body tense behind me, his shoulders tightening, the muscles in his arms stiffening. He was willing to keep me on Earth, but he wasn't willing to tie me to Purgatory for all eternity.

I dropped the conversation, realizing we were both aiming for different things with different outcomes. But with his lips by my ear again, his breath hot on my skin, he whispered, "I will never guide you in the wrong direction."

And I believed him. I trusted him with everything in me, with all of my mind, body, and soul, and I knew he was being honest. I knew he would never lead me astray.

But I ached for that promise, the sacred vow of committing myself to something bigger. Something that was fact and truth, something I could physically see with my own eyes.

Something I had fallen in love with, with or without the ties to the afterlife.

My gaze traveled back to the steady rainfall against the window. The sound was soothing, the sight was relaxing, and I found myself slipping deeper into Caius' embrace. The warm water and floating flower petals were only adding to the serenity.

And with that, I knew there was nowhere else I could imagine myself.

"Caius," I began. I turned my body slightly, angling myself so my back was no longer pressed against him, but against the side of the tub instead. His grey eyes met mine as his arms continued to rest against my skin, the water softly lapping against us, and I could tell that our gazes were no longer simple. He could read me, just like I could read him, and there were three words I so badly wanted to say.

"I know," he replied before I had a chance to speak. His hand moved to tuck a stray lock of hair behind my ear. "I do, too."

The beat of my heart jumped at the underlying admission. It was there, swirling around us, the exhilarating feelings and emotions with no chance of settling.

Without thinking, I leaned up and kissed him, letting the action lead my emotions. His hands cupped my face as he kissed me back.

Celeste

The coffee shop needed me for a double shift, so by the time I clocked out, I was exhausted. My feet were aching, my back was tight, and all I wanted to do was fall into Caius' silk sheets. Maybe take a bath first.

Oh, yeah. Definitely a bath.

Turning onto the fog-covered road, I didn't bother to concentrate. My hands knew the way, and at this point, it was all muscle memory.

That is, until a car faced me head-on, the headlights barely breaking through the thick white cloud between us. I slammed on my brakes, silently hoping the car could see me and do the same.

Thankfully, whoever was driving took notice. But instead of going around me and continuing on, the person in the car got out and looked to the ground, trying to see how much room they had on the road.

I rolled down my window, and fog instantly seeped into my car. "If you move a little to your right, you'll be able to get around me," I said, unable to fully see who I was talking to. The person was tall, and had the silhouette of a man, but those were the only features I could make out.

But within seconds, any secrecies of the person's identity vanished.

"Celeste?"

The man's voice broke through the fog and found its way to me.

I knew that voice.

Shit.

I know who that is.

Shit shit shit shit.

I squeezed my eyes shut, hoping to somehow avoid the conversation I knew was about to happen.

"Celeste, is that you?"

Gripping the steering wheel, I kept my lips tight, hoping he would magically forget it was me in the car in front of him.

But the darkened figure walked toward me and my car, and as he filtered his way through the fog, I could see him clearly.

"Hi, Uncle Lucas."

"What the hell are you doing here?" he asked, leaning on my open window frame.

I didn't answer. Instead, I looked up to him with lost eyes, knowing that he didn't *need* my answer.

"Celeste, *damn it.*" Uncle Lucas wiped a hand down his face. "Your dad is gonna kill me."

I shook my head. "No. It's fine. It's fine, right?"

Uncle Lucas gave no verbal response as he stared down at the pavement below, unable to make eye contact with me.

"It's fine," I repeated.

More silence swirled between us as Uncle Lucas refused to leave my car. His hands remained planted on the frame, gripping tight as his decisions were left in the tension.

"What are you doing here?" he asked again in a heavy whisper. "This isn't…" his voice trailed off, then picked back up. "This isn't a place you should be."

"I know," I admitted. He was right, but wrong at the same time. He didn't know what my mind had been through recently, and he didn't know where I stood with all the information I had.

I could tell him that I was only here to visit Uncle Russ, but we both knew it was a lie. Not only has it been weeks, maybe even months, since I've visited my uncle's mausoleum, but we also saw each other at the Open House party. It's not even worth it to pretend like there was any other reason to be here, other than the truth.

He knew it. I knew it.

"I came here to tell him I'm no longer interested," Uncle Lucas stated, as if he was following the same mind track as me. "I couldn't call or anything, obviously, so I had to drive my ass up here and do it myself."

My eyes met his in a nervous glare. This was the first time either one of us gave up the façade, admitting to the truth of the situation out loud.

No vague words, no insinuation, no alluding.

Only truthfulness.

"I hope you're doing the same, Celeste. Whatever it is you have going on here…"

Unable to finish his sentence, he turned his head to the side, squinting his eyes as he tried to look up the hill.

"You're a big girl, Cel, and I can't tell you what to do. No matter what, you'll always have a good head on your shoulders. Don't fuck that up because of this."

My heart sank a bit at his vulnerability.

But he doesn't know the complete truth.

"Just… don't."

He doesn't know that I've *tried* to commit my soul to Purgatory.

Caius simply won't let me.

"I love you, Celeste. Your family loves you."

I nodded, choking back sudden emotion. "I know."

"Please, think with your head and not just your heart, okay?"

I nodded because that's all I could do. I couldn't tell him what I wanted because I wasn't sure if it was even attainable.

Uncle Lucas reached through the window to give my shoulder a gentle squeeze, then walked through the fog back to his car. I watched as he slowly maneuvered his way around my car, the heavy mist making any efforts to wave goodbye through the window futile.

I exhaled a deep, long breath.

Celeste

The door to Caius' office was open slightly, and as I made my way down the windowed hallway, I could see a patch of light filtering through the gap. When I reached the door, I could hear the soft crackle of the fireplace, and I gently pushed the door open to see the flames dancing behind him. He didn't look up from whatever he was reading, with his elbows propped up on the surface and one hand running through his dark hair. I snuck in as quietly as I could, gently clicking the door closed behind me.

Without looking up, he muttered, "About time."

I grinned from ear to ear as I approached his side of the desk. He dropped his arms and swiveled his chair in my direction, meeting me as my body found his.

"I've been waiting for you," he rasped as his hands found the back of my legs, bringing them up onto his lap. I placed a knee on each side, straddling him, and I could feel Caius' hands find their way to my ass. He palmed me, gripping me through my dark jeans with his large hands and long fingers.

"Double shift?" he asked.

I nodded in response to him. "You talked to my uncle?" I inquired, tilting my head to the side as I trailed a finger vertically down the left side of his neck.

Caius nodded, and I could tell he was more focused on where my touch was headed rather than where the conversation was going. When he didn't elaborate, I spoke again.

"What made him change his mind?"

Caius shrugged. "Sometimes it's just not a good fit."

"He didn't give a real reason why?"

"No."

I thought back to the car, when Uncle Lucas made it known that he was concerned for me.

Maybe his family was the reason why he changed his mind.

Maybe *I* was the reason.

Whatever it may be, it was over now, and I could put that problem out of my mind permanently.

Turning back to the sight of Caius' body, I pressed my thighs down onto his lap just a little bit harder, enough to bring his full focus back to me.

His hands roamed all over my backside, but always found their way back to the curves of my ass.

Instinctively, I rolled my hips against his growing erection, forcing a low rumble to escape from his throat. My lips found his in a welcoming embrace, and my tongue slid into his mouth in search for him. The kisses grew heavier, our touches increased in their heat, and the lust was only beginning.

Caius moved his hands to the bottom of my white shirt, lifting the hem so slightly, and slid his hands onto my bare skin. A chill ran over my entire being at his brush.

Just as he was about to move my shirt over my head, the door to the office swung open. Caius and I both turned to look.

"Fuck, sorry. I should've knocked." Ace came bounding in, his blonde, shaggy hair swaying with each step.

"What, Ace?" Caius snipped, clearly aggravated at the interruption.

Ace said nothing, but instead looked over his shoulder to the monitor on the wall. We followed his gaze and noticed a silver car pulling up to the front door of the house.

"Shit," Caius spoke under his breath.

I looked from the screen, to Caius, then back to the screen. "Who is that?"

"What do you want me to do?" Ace asked, both of them ignoring my question.

With his hands still under my shirt, resting on my bare skin, Caius shook his head. "Nothing. Let him say whatever he needs to get off his chest."

Ace gave a half turn, about to leave, before turning back to Caius. "Why do you let him in? Why do you let him speak to you like this?"

And that's when I figured out who they were talking about. *Amadeus.*

Caius shrugged. "Because if I'm his punching bag, then at least it stays here. He can get it all out in the open and keep his mouth shut when he leaves."

"What, like a fucking therapy session?" Ace replied, heavy in his sarcasm.

"So far, it's worked," Caius said, his eyes moving back to the screen. Amadeus got out of the car, locked it, and walked up to the front door. We watched as Amadeus jiggled the locked handle, unable to get in. Caius reached under his desk and pressed a hidden button, activating a security feature to unlock the door. But with his hand hidden, I heard him grab something else. Metal clanked on the underside of the desk, and I knew what he was going for.

My eyes briefly met Caius' as he tucked a gun in the back waistband of his pants.

Amadeus pushed open the door and stepped inside.

I crawled backward off Caius' lap and began to walk away from the desk, until Caius grabbed my hand and pulled me back. He stood to his feet and glared at me.

"Stay with me," he commanded, his focus piercing into me, drilling an unease into my body. I nodded in agreement.

Caius nodded to Ace. "You stay here, too."

"You sure?" Ace asked. "If he sees all of us here, he might not want to talk."

"It's fine," Caius assured, but I could tell it wasn't fine. There was a waver in his voice, a hint of edge in his throat. I took note, making sure to keep his apprehension in the back of my mind.

After a minute, I could hear footsteps approaching the door, and without warning, the door busted open. Amadeus stumbled in, his black hair greasy and untamed, his cheeks sunken in, and his eyes hollowed with deep, purple circles.

"Fuck, Dey, are you on some shit? What is wrong with you?" Caius asked, more angry than concerned.

Amadeus shook his head in distrust. "Nothing's wrong with *me*," he spit out. "What's wrong with *you*? How many offers will it take for you to give this place up?"

Offers. He was mad about Caius denying *offers.*

As if taking one of the offers would change anything about what Purgatory is. It would only change the hands it belonged to.

Caius refused to answer the question. Instead, his hand found the small of my back in an act of protection.

Amadeus' eyes scanned each of us individually. When his gaze landed on me, his eyes narrowed, and his head cocked to the side.

"You?" he spoke, verifying his memory of me. "You're the one from the party."

Flashes of the party sparked in my mind. The memory of me hearing Amadeus out and listening to everything he had to say. The way he stood on the chair, the knife and champagne in hand, and the way he looked so much better back then than he does now.

So, what happened in that span of time?

He took a few steps toward the desk, but Ace stepped over, blocking him from getting any closer.

"Ace," he smiled warmly, even though there was clearly no love in his voice. "How you doin', buddy? You're still stuck under Caius' thumb around here? Does he at least pay you well?"

Ace placed a palm on Amadeus' chest, adding pressure and making him stumble.

"Dey, you need to step back," Ace warned, and Amadeus brushed off his request.

"Remember when we used to sneak out back?" Amadeus asked Ace, still staring at him. "You know, go out to the edge of the property, behind the Mason Mausoleum and get so shit-faced that we would pass out until fucking noon the next day? We would wake up drenched from the rain—and, I don't know—it sobered us, don't you think?"

"Why are you here?" Caius interrupted, and Amadeus turned back to him.

"Because, brother," he sneered, "I'm done letting this shitty place sit in my conscience." He lifted his hand, revealing a shiny object glinting in the light, reflecting a white beam.

It was a knife.

The same knife he had at the party, the one he used to open the bottle of champagne.

He must've grabbed it from the kitchen before coming to the office.

I took a sharp inhale at the sight, and I could feel Caius' hand snake around my hip, gripping me. But even though I knew he was trying to protect me, to shield me, a part of me didn't want it.

Or maybe I felt as if I didn't need it because I understood Amadeus.

I understood the feeling of disbelief. Hesitancy. Skepticism. I was there for so long.

My hand found Caius', and I gave him a soft squeeze before forcing his hand off my hip. We both looked at each other, his concerned, confused stare meeting my hopeful one.

"I get it," I began, turning to face Amadeus. "I felt the same way, too."

All three men turned to look at me as I stepped out from behind the desk. I walked slowly toward Amadeus, who was still situated behind Ace.

"When I first figured out what *this* was—*all of this*—I didn't believe it. Even though I saw it with my own eyes, I still didn't believe it. And then, when I accepted it for what it really was, I didn't agree with it, just like you."

The look in Amadeus' eyes softened, so I took another step forward.

"Just like your parents, my uncle is here, and I had a very hard time accepting the fact that he wanted this. From what I know, he was such a good man, and the thought of him wanting this made my stomach turn. I thought he deserved better."

I glanced over my shoulder to Caius, who looked ready to jump over the desk and grab me. He wanted to save me, I could tell, but right now, I needed him to stay put.

"But, Dey," I looked back at him. "Can I call you that? Dey?"

He gave no response, so I continued.

"There is so much more to it than I could've imagined. There's life here every single night. There's thought in each decision. There's confidence and hope in each agreement. This isn't just an easy way out. These are people's lives we are dealing with here. This is their eternal soul in the balance."

Amadeus' face remained neutral as I took one final step toward him. Ace shifted to the side, and I could feel him watching us, waiting to react at the jump if necessary.

"Death is inevitable, Dey. We all know that. But you know what's avoidable? Fearing death because of the unknowns of the afterlife. There's no reason to be scared when you know peace is waiting for you on the other side."

Right as the last word left my lips, Amadeus grabbed my arm and pulled me into him. In a swift movement, he spun me around so my back was against his heated chest, then brought the knife up to my throat.

Both Ace and Caius made moves to come for me, but Amadeus hissed from over my shoulder.

"Don't you fucking dare come any closer, or I'll slice her throat open."

Ace held his hands up in surrender. My eyes met Caius', who looked absolutely fucking terrified. But then his eyes moved to Amadeus', and suddenly, the fear was gone. His gaze turned to stone as he watched his own brother hold a knife to my neck.

"You want to talk to me in that condescending tone?" Amadeus asked me through gritted teeth. "You think I'm ignorant? You want to act as if I didn't *live* here for the majority of my life? Like I wasn't forced to grow the fuck up here?"

I swallowed down a small, sudden lump of nerves. Half of me panicked, but the other half was oddly calm. I knew Amadeus was passionate about taking Purgatory down, or at least forcing everyone to abandon it, but I firmly believed that he would never truly act on it.

Although my mind was trying to think rationally, my body was not. I held my breath deep in my lungs, careful to not do anything that would cause my throat to press against the blade.

"Dey, I swear to *fucking* God—"

"*What*, Cai? You talk to God now? You guys are finally on good terms?"

Caius wasn't taking any of Dey's shit. Not now. I watched as he clenched his jaw so hard, his teeth looked like they could break behind his cheeks.

With his arms still tightly wrapped around me, Amadeus pulled me closer, forcing my back to bend slightly. As much as I hated to admit it, his body felt similar to Caius'. They had the same hard chest and strong arms, but there was no comfort with Amadeus. Only captivity.

His mouth leaned in close to my ear, and he whispered quietly enough where the others couldn't hear him.

"What has he done to you?" he asked, referring to Caius, his words coated with a light layer of sympathy. "You're not the same person from the party. He has *ruined* you."

"Fuck off," I mumbled in return.

"Are you promised here, too, little Miss Dalmatian? Did you sign your soul to the Grey Devil?"

"You better watch your goddamn mouth, Dey," Caius barked, but Amadeus ignored him.

"Huh? You got a cut on your hand? Let me see."

"No," I replied, keeping my hands low. I didn't want to give him any ounce of information, even if it could benefit me or relieve this situation.

Ace moved to step closer, and Amadeus pushed the steel harder against my throat in retaliation. Ace froze.

"Amadeus, you better let her *the fuck* go, right *fucking now.*" Caius' voice sounded more broken with each word he spoke, and that broke *me.* I couldn't bear to meet Caius' eyes now, in the chance that my strong stance would completely crumble.

"You know," I added, my body gaining composure as we all ignored Caius, "you come here a lot for a guy who doesn't want anything to do with this."

"What good would I be if I wanted to put a stop to something but didn't act on it? There's not much I can do without coming here. I can't call, I can't text, I can't even fucking email."

"Dey," Caius spoke, his voice softer this time. "You need to let her go. We can talk about this."

"Yeah, okay," Amadeus let out a dry laugh. "You're only saying that because of *this.*" Amadeus flashed the knife, letting it catch the light's reflection as he added a small amount of pressure to my windpipe.

"No, I'm not, Dey. You got my attention, now let's talk about it."

The sincerity in Caius' voice had me choking back an onset of tears. If he was nervous, he was hiding it well, but I couldn't bring myself to look at him and check. My focus remained on the steel blade under my chin, and I could feel Amadeus tense behind me. There was a hesitation at Caius' words, I could feel it, but I could also feel some sort of consideration.

Amadeus' grip on me loosened, but only by a fraction. The arm that was tightly wrapped around my torso eased up slightly, but it was enough to give me breathing room.

And in that newfound freedom, I knew what I had to do.

Run.

Run like the first time I saw the ghosts. Run as if I saw my uncle's spirit for the first time again, and that's all my body wanted to do.

Run.

I finally looked up to Caius, whose gaze never strayed away from me. I sent a plea to him, to catch me when I came running. With a barely noticeable nod to me, I knew he was aware of what I was about to do.

So, with all my might, I attempted to slip out of Amadeus' hold and run to Caius.

But the second he felt me move, his arm around my torso tightened again.

And as he struggled to keep me flush against him, he subconsciously moved the hand holding the knife to my abdomen. Between the rush of my fight and the strength of his reaction, the blade turned its angle against me just perfectly.

White hot pain seared through the middle of my stomach. I stopped moving and looked down to see the handle of the knife sticking out of my body like an extra limb. Red liquid began to seep through my white shirt, and I knew.

I just knew.

Caius

"_No!_" A roar blasted out through my lungs before I could stop it. A series of events happened all at once in record time. Not a single moment was wasted as Ace tackled Amadeus, pinned him to the ground, and locked him in a secure hold. Celeste immediately grew ghostly pale as she fell to the ground. I rushed out from behind the desk, unable to make it to her in time before her body landed with a loud thud on the floor. I kneeled down by her side.

"Oh, God," Amadeus mumbled in Ace's chokehold. "Oh… God… What have I done? I didn't mean to…"

With a quick scan over Celeste, I knew this wasn't good. Her blood was pouring out of her stomach, and she was fading out quickly. I cradled her head as she lay on the floor, her arms and legs sprawled out in different directions. She blinked at me slowly, but it was enough for me to know she was still somewhat conscious.

Not a single bone in my body was hesitant as I pulled my gun out from my waistband, aimed it at Amadeus' forehead, and shot him. The bullet went clean through his skull, immediately killing him. Brain splatter and fresh blood lined the wall next to Ace, who only slightly winced at the loud crack of the gun.

Ace released Amadeus, who laid limp on the floor. I placed my gun back in my waistband.

"Celeste," I said, turning back to her. "Celeste, baby, I need you to focus on me."

Her lips began to pale, and her body was weakening. Her eyelids started to move slower, and her blinks were growing heavier as her vision began losing focus. I pressed a gentle hand to the wound in her stomach, careful to keep the knife in its place. Within seconds, my entire hand was saturated in thick, heavy blood.

"Call Doctor Paulson," I commanded Ace. "Get him in here, *now*. And get Father Nicholas."

A light groan slipped from Celeste's colorless lips.

"Caius…" Ace began hesitantly.

"Now," I roared in return.

I could see Ace shake his head from the corner of my eye. *"Caius."*

I tore my gaze away from Celeste to look at Ace, who remained sitting on the floor beside me. His eyes were full of sorrow, a look that I knew I could not accept.

"By the time they get here…"

"No," I shook my head again, my soul in complete denial, and returned my focus to Celeste. "No. You have to stay. Come on, baby. *Stay.*"

With one hand still cradling the base of her skull, my other hand slipped between her shoulder blades. I lifted her up, careful not to add more pressure to her wound, letting her dark hair fall over my arms.

Bile began to rise in my throat when I realized that Ace was right. He would have to leave the property and drive until his phone got service. That in itself takes longer than it should.

There's no way help would come in time.

I could feel my chest begin to shatter.

"Keep me," Celeste whispered with all the breath left in her lungs.

"No, Celeste. You're going to be fine. You're not going anywhere."

My words deceived me as I was unable to believe my own lies. Based on the amount of blood at my knees and her slowing pulse, I knew my words to her were hollow. And as much as I wanted to deny it, I knew I only had so much time to make a decision.

She wanted me to keep her here.

I would do anything to honor her request. But I know if I don't listen to her, she will go somewhere better than here. She will be happy in her own Paradise, away from here.

But fuck, the selfish side wants her with me.

Forever.

"Please, Caius."

Just like the first time she ever said it, the sound of my name on her lips completely ripped me apart.

I could feel Ace at my back, and even if he was trying to give me space, there was an added pressure intensifying. He was waiting for me to figure out my next move.

But *I* didn't even know what my plan was. I needed time to think, but time was the only thing I didn't have right now.

Celeste's breathing was slowing down, blood was continuing to pool at my knees, and her eyes fluttered closed.

Fuck.

With impending sorrow building in my chest, it took all my strength to grumble out my aching words. *"Stay awake, Meum Caelum."*

The shattered grip in my voice was firm as I tried to keep my composure. All I wanted to do was crumble, lay on the floor with her, and breathe her in, but I couldn't.

I knew what I had to do.

"Stay with her," I turned to Ace. "Do not let her go. Do whatever it takes to keep her conscious."

Ace nodded to me in confirmation. I moved my arms out from under her and positioned her head gently on the floor, but it took everything in me to move to stand. I couldn't find it in me to tear myself away from her. The entire essence of my being felt attached to her in this state, and every other state.

But with my knees covered in her fresh, innocent blood, I forced myself to get up.

And once I was standing, looking down at her rapidly declining body, rage overtook me.

I ran to the bookshelf on the far side wall and found the boxes of vials. I tore open the lid, tossed it aside, and dumped out the small containers. *Glass shattered on the floor,* releasing all the blood that was collected over time.

Everyone who was promised here was promised here no longer.

Including her uncle.

Including my parents.

Blood, old and new, lay in thick puddles on the floor, oxidizing in the fresh air. Every single vial was broken under my feet.

Except for one.

The empty vial that was for *her.*

I shoved it in my pants pocket.

Then, I grabbed the other set of boxes on the shelves, ripped them open, and made my way to the fireplace.

I knew I had to *burn every paper with the deal.*

I gripped handfuls of paper and threw them into the fire. Old, stiff handprints curled in the flames in front of me. I threw in more, and more, and more, until every shred of bloodied paper was ash. My breath struggled to keep steady as I threw the last box to the side.

There were two final papers that were never in a box. One with *my* bloody handprint and signature from about six years ago, from a rare drunken night with Dey. Although we both committed ourselves on paper, we never went all the way through with it and filled any vials.

I kept my paper and destroyed his after my parents died.

The other paper had *only* a signature from about six weeks ago, and I never let a drop of blood on it.

They both resided in a drawer in my desk, tucked away from eyesight.

I reached down and pulled them out. Along with the gun that was tucked against my back, I left the bloodied page on the desk and paid it no mind. Instead, my eyes fixated on the one with the blank space and scribbled signature at the bottom.

Heartache crept up into my throat as I vacantly stared at the white paper. *Fuck, I don't want to do it.*

Grabbing the paper, I walked back to Celeste and Ace. He had her resting on his leg, propping her up in comfort as red blood covered the front of his thighs. He looked up at me and nodded, and I nodded in return, kneeling down and meeting him at eye level.

"Ace," I started, my voice unsteady. "This is yours."

"What is?"

"This."

I nodded my chin toward the window, and his eyes peered into mine, catching my implication but still unsure if I was serious.

"This is all yours. I trust you more than I trust anyone."

Ace remained motionless and expressionless as I continued.

"After my parents died, and after everything fell into my hands, I created a will of my own. If anything were to happen, this was always meant to go to you."

Stillness blanketed the room as Ace made no moves to respond.

"All I ask is that you take care of it. Live here. Start a family here. Keep it in *your* family. Keep it with Mel, if she even wants it. And don't accept any more souls."

His eyes widened at my requests. "What do you mean, Cai?" Nerves and fear coated his tone. "This is yours. You own it."

I shook my head. "Not anymore."

And I meant it. Every part of me felt dead, and there was nothing in this world that could change that.

Grabbing Celeste's hand, I could feel her heat dissipating. What once was a hand that held my own was now a hand that predicted her eternal future.

A future she asked for in her final, fatal words, and I'd be damned if I didn't give her what she wanted.

"I want you to know, Celeste, I'll give you everything you want. Anything, it's yours."

The memory of my words rang through my head as I gently moved her hand to her stomach, coating the skin in her fresh, vibrant blood. Her delicate fingers, ones that previously plucked flower petals, waved through warm bath water, and grazed upon my cheek, now rested in the liquid that committed her to me.

No. Not me. Ace.

Laying the paper on my thigh, I brought her hand to it and pressed it down, creating a perfect, clear print.

I exhaled and moved her hand down to her side. Looking back at Ace, who was still in a confused state of shock, I handed him the paper.

"Keep it," I ordered calmly and seriously, referring to more than just the paper in his hand and the paper on the desk. Ace gave a single nod.

My one arm moved under Celeste's upper back while the other slid in under her knees. I lifted her, standing to my feet, sure to keep her cradled and comfortable. A hiss of air squeezed out of her as I positioned her firmly against my chest.

I turned to leave my office when I heard Ace at my back.

"Cai…"

I ignored him as I walked down the windowed hallway, the heavy rain tapping the glass as I headed to the stairs.

Caius

As I ascended the steps, I could feel the atmosphere around me changing. As the veil was thinning, the air was thickening. Carrying Celeste in my arms, I could feel her body fall completely limp as her blood trailed under me. The red liquid was sliding down my pants, past my shoes, and onto the hardwood floor below. Her breathing was slow, shallow, and the final sign that there wasn't much time left.

But as I landed on the top step, the feeling hit me. Each step had me closer to the end. I was walking in the space between life and death.

Between Earth and Purgatory.

Between her life and mine.

The Between.

Mindlessly, I found myself carrying her to my bedroom. I swung open the door, walked through the room, and headed to the bathroom.

Her favorite room.

I refused to flick on the lights as we entered the bathroom. More than enough natural light was filtering in from the clouded skies, bouncing off the leafy trees, illuminating the room in a subtle green hue.

I walked to the bathtub and turned on the water, keeping Celeste in the balance of my arms as I did so.

The water was perfectly warmer than normal, just as she liked it.

As the tub was filling, I kneeled down on the floor, letting Celeste rest on my thighs. I pulled out the vial from my pocket and opened it.

Celeste's head tilted back as she slipped out of consciousness. I could see the heartbeat in her throat, as faint and slow as it may be. Her body was giving up the fight.

I pressed the small glass container next to the knife that still protruded from her stomach. Her blood pooled out of the wound, and I was able to catch enough to fill half the vial.

I placed the lid back on and held the tube tight in my palm.

Lifting her back up, I stood to my feet and looked at the tub. It was half filled. I slipped off my shoes and stepped into the water.

Warmth surrounded my ankles, but I couldn't feel it. All I could feel was the numbness flowing through me, overtaking me as I remained in the Between.

I moved to sit in the water, the levels rising from our added volume. I turned the faucet off.

Rain continued to tap against the window in a soundtrack to the last moments.

Red water moved in waves against the porcelain as her blood curled in an instant mixture.

She rested against me, my arms still cradling her as I stared at her face.

It was not too long ago that we were in this exact position. But now, the flower petals that floated on the surface were replaced with streams of blood, and her soft-spoken words were replaced with shallow breaths teetering on the brink of finality.

"Caius…"

"I know. I do, too."

Leaning forward, I kissed the three that lined her face. My lips lingered on her cold skin as our clothes soaked in the warm water.

"I love you, *Meum Caelum.*"

My Heaven.

As I spoke those words, I could feel her exhale her final breath under my kiss. Her skin stilled, her lips froze, and her light pulse stopped. The ache in my throat grew heavy at the permanence of it all.

She was gone.

I couldn't bring myself to pull my lips away as my arms remained around her in a temporary tomb. I was in a state of denial, and I wanted to be in this moment forever. I wanted *her* forever.

Life doesn't play out the way you want it to.

But death can.

Finally tearing my lips away from her, I gathered the strength to look at her. She was lifeless, she was cold, she was limp, but she was still so fucking beautiful.

The sight of her ripped me to pieces. My insides felt like they were torn apart by a chainsaw, never to be fixed again. With her soul gone, I no longer had life.

What's a soul?

I closed my eyes, and suddenly, I was able to see the tilt of her head at my question.

The first question I ever asked her.

Her curiosity always got the best of her.

Her fear never outweighed her grief.

Her mind and her choices were all her own.

Even her final one.

Opening my eyes, I looked down at her stomach. The knife was still protruding, the handle was sticking out of the water, the blade remained buried deep. Placing the vial between my teeth, I pulled the knife out of her stomach, forcing more blood to spill out into the water.

There was no hesitation in what I was about to do.

I slid my arm out from under Celeste, whose back was still against the side of the tub. I brought the bladed steel to the inside of my forearm, pressed down, and slid vertically upward. The inked skin separated, instantly drawing a heavy flow of blood.

My brows furrowed as I switched arms. With the knife in my other hand, I mirrored the action, opening that forearm as well.

I dropped the blade into the water and didn't think about it again.

Grabbing the vial from between my teeth, I quickly opened it and held it under one of my bleeding arms. The blood trickled down into the glass tube, quickly filling it to the top. I pushed the lid back on and carefully placed it on the bathroom floor next to the tub.

For as long as I've known about Purgatory, and for as long as I've been involved in it, I've never known anyone to mix blood. I don't know if it had ever been attempted, and I wasn't sure if it was going to work.

But there's no fucking way I wasn't going to try.

I didn't know if I was going about this the right way, but this was how my gut was telling me to do it. Then again, there were so many variables that I couldn't afford to consider right now.

The only thing I knew was that I felt completely powerless in this situation. And if I could bring myself to be with her again, that's the best way I can get my power back.

Moving my bleeding arm under Celeste, I pulled her close to my chest. Both of my arms rested under the surface of the water, and soon, the color went from a bright red to a dark crimson.

This was it. This was the end of the balance.

I cradled her lifeless body as I could feel myself fading. Black stars began to line my vision, and my head felt light. My mouth went dry, and it was getting harder to breathe.

But I didn't fight it. I didn't try to keep my strength.

I closed my eyes, rested my head on top of Celeste's, and breathed her in.

I inhaled her scent one final time before falling into the void.

A white flower petal slipped between my fingertips.

Snapdragon. Purity. Innocence.

I grinned at its beauty. It was growing tall, taller than I remember it being before.

I slid down the row to the next set of flowers, feeling all the soft, velvet material brushing under the pads of my fingers.

I found my way to the back of the greenhouse, approaching the glass door. I opened it slowly, letting the new wave of humidity hit me in full force.

I stepped through, making my way to the inground, circular pond. The water was its normal magical teal color, and I found myself in awe of the crystalized beauty. The surface of the water was still, it was calm, and it was tranquil. My gaze moved up to all the greenery woven throughout the room and also to the new flowers that decided to find their way into the mix.

Roses. Marigolds. *Carnations.*

The sight of those ones made my grin spread wide. They were so beautiful, so stunning, so elegant. I found myself studying these flowers more than any other.

They also looked healthier than ever, with the mist dotting the leaves, the buds blossoming, and the sunrays feeding them through the glass windows. I could feel the heat on the side of my face as I watched the flowers drink the water from the sprinkler above.

But then it hit me.

Sun.

I turned to look up and out the roof of the greenhouse. Sure enough, the sun was beaming down on me, on the building, and on the plants.

"What?" I whispered to myself. There was no rain, there were no clouds, there was no gloom.

My knees grew weak as I sprinted out of the pond room, weaved through the rows of flowers, and made it to the door. I pulled it open and ran outside. The sun warmed my skin like a beautiful spring day, and I had to shield my eyes as I looked up to the sky. It was a beautiful blue with no cloud in sight. My breath felt stuck in my lungs as I stood there, confused, unsure if I was dreaming or not.

I had to be dreaming. Right?

There was never sun in Purgatory. Only rain.

"For you," a voice called to my side, and I dropped my hand to turn and look.

My heart fell to the pit of my stomach at the sight of him.

Caius.

I don't know why, but the sight of him had my insides screaming in relief. He was my comfort, my safety, my soul. And to see him here—*with me*—made me realize that I was scared without knowing it. I didn't notice that I was alone until I wasn't.

I ran to him, wrapping my arms around his neck the second I reached him. His arms embraced me as well, and I could feel him bury his face in the crook of my neck, planting gentle kisses on the exposed skin.

Even though I didn't want to let him go, I managed to pull away just enough to ask a question.

"How is this possible? How is the sun out right now?"

His answer was simple. "Because you always wanted the sun here."

"But…" I said, still confused. "How?"

"You want the sun, I give you the sun."

With one arm still around his neck, I slightly turned to look up at the sky. The warmth on my skin felt incredible, but something was off. A piece of me felt different. This whole situation felt… different.

Why do I feel different?

The change in scenery had me pausing, along with the heat on my skin. And the fact that I was here, even though I don't remember coming here, had me momentarily confused.

And my hands on Caius felt more like a memory than my reality.

This isn't how I know Purgatory.

I looked back at Caius, who still had his arms snaked around my hips. I studied the feeling of his body warm against mine, and in that moment, I knew that was the only warmth I wanted. *Needed.*

But why can I feel his warmth?

"Give me the rain back," I forced out with a smile, which he gladly returned.

With a quick snap of his fingers, the skies turned a deep grey, and heavy rain clouds appeared from nowhere. A drop of rain landed on my cheek, then another on my hand, and soon, the rain was in a consistent downpour.

This was the Purgatory I was more than familiar with. Any hesitancy left in my body was buried beneath my desire to stay with him.

For eternity.

I wrapped my arms around Caius again, letting the rainfall drown me. I kissed him, and the heat of his lips on mine filled my entire body.

"You and me, *Meum Caelum*," he whispered against my lips. "It's only us."

And I knew, right then and there, *there is nothing better than this.*